'Give up, Rhys. All the other women you've known may have fallen at your feet, but I'm not going to.' Something flickered across his face and, suddenly, Meredith was convinced she was right.

'You hoped I was going to find you irresistible and you simply can't get over the fact that I'm completely indifferent to you!'

'Is that a fact?' Rhys said. Taking hold of her by the forearms, he pulled her none too gently to his chest.

'Let go of me!' Meredith demanded.

'Why, you're trembling!' Rhys exclaimed softly, husky laughter edging his words. 'Didn't you just say you were totally indifferent to me?'

'I . . . I'm not indifferent. I actively dislike you!' she flashed breathlessly, trying to free herself. 'You're arrogant and conceited and you think every woman is longing to have an affair with you!'

'If your luck holds you just might be one of them,' he said.

A MATCH FOR MEREDITH

BY

JENNY ARDEN

MILLS & BOON LIMITED
ETON HOUSE   18-24 PARADISE ROAD
RICHMOND   SURREY   TW9 1SR

*First published in Great Britain 1991
by Mills & Boon Limited*

© Jenny Arden 1991

*Australian copyright 1991
Philippine copyright 1992
This edition 1992*

ISBN 0 263 77434 1

*Set in Times Roman 11½ on 12 pt.
01-9202-45943 C*

Made and printed in Great Britain

CHAPTER ONE

IT WAS ironic, Meredith thought. Not three months ago Trefor had been pressurising her to marry him. Yet now, when she'd say yes without hesitation, he seemed quite content with their relationship as it stood.

A faint furrow creased her brow as she continued along the beautiful stretch of empty beach which formed part of Cardigan Bay. Her black mongrel bounded ahead of her. She held her leather sandals in her hand.

The tide was out and to a chance watcher driving along the quiet coast road she made a solitary and evocative figure. Her long flame-coloured hair blew about her shoulders; her bright skirt dipped and flared in the breeze. There was something pagan and unfettered about her movements as she splashed through the wavelets, a half-tamed quality that singled her out as different and which men invariably found a challenge.

Close to, with her flaming Titian hair and flawless ivory skin, she was even more striking. Her winged dark brows were well marked, her cheekbones high and her chin pointed. But it was her eyes that held the key to her elfin charm. Fringed with long, auburn-tipped lashes, they held lights of their own in their fascinating amber depths.

She halted and stood staring out at the vastness of the shimmering blue bay. She felt restless and unsettled. The cry of the gulls came in sharp keening volleys and then faded, leaving only the ceaseless call of the sea.

Even though her feelings had stolen up on her gradually, she believed she loved Trefor. When he'd first started dating her there'd been no doubt that he was the pursuer and she the pursued. He'd courted her as ardently as any woman could have wished until a couple of months ago. Now, though she could scarcely accuse him of neglecting her, he seemed to be taking their relationship for granted and she wasn't sure what she should do about it.

Her dog trotted up to her and pushed his nose into her hand, demanding that she take notice of him. She bent down and pulled his ears affectionately.

'If only...' she began, voicing her thoughts aloud, and then broke off with a sigh.

There was no point wishing Trefor had timed his proposal differently.

She straightened up and glanced at her watch. Generally a long walk along the beach with the breeze tugging at her hair made her feel content, at one with the sea, the sky and the mountains. But today the charm hadn't worked. She still felt vaguely unsettled.

She would have walked on to the next breakwater if time had allowed. But her father was giving a dinner party that evening and she knew that Margred, his housekeeper, would appreciate some help.

She had left her Peugeot parked by the sea wall. Calling to Jet to follow her, she headed up the beach towards it. She noticed that she had caught the sun a little.

She drove with the car windows open. The massive mountains on either side of the estuary road were turned to splendour by the late afternoon sun. The dark conifers rose in their massed ranks to meet the scree-scarred summits, while below her she could glimpse the river that curved lazily, ripples of light dancing off its wide expanse.

Deciding to take a short cut, she turned off the main road on to one of the farm tracks. It was poorly surfaced and climbed steeply over the broad shoulders of the mountains, dropping down into Bryn Uchel just below the bridge.

Soon she was up among the rocky outcrops. The wall on either side of the track petered out. Some sheep cropping the grass by the roadside broke into a run, startled by the approach of her car. As she passed them they veered off on to the rough grazing land that was mottled with patches of coarse juncus grass.

The track was used, in general, only by farm vehicles, so she was surprised when a maroon Jaguar XJ6 came into sight. It was hardly the kind of car for such a rough road.

There was a passing point some distance further back up the road but from the way the other car was coming towards her, keeping to the crown of the track, its driver clearly intended forcing her to reverse into it. The stranger's arrogance nettled her. It was no more his right of way than it was hers.

Her mouth tightening a little with defiance, she drove on. She fully expected that when the other driver saw she wasn't going to give to him he would pull in tightly at the side of the track, allowing her to drive past. Instead, to her annoyance, the Jaguar continued to approach and she was obliged to brake.

The Jaguar likewise drew to a halt. She gave the driver, a strong-featured dark-haired man, a hostile glare. In reply he quirked a sardonic eyebrow at her. His mock salute at her stubbornness, which meant neither of them could now proceed, antagonised her. Yet, even so, she might have put her Peugeot into reverse had he not had the audacity to lift a laconic hand from the wheel, motioning her to back up.

'Arrogant pig,' she muttered under her breath.

Her eyes went to the grassy bank on her side of the track. If she encroached on it she would, she judged, have just enough room to edge past the stationary Jaguar. It was going to allow her no margin for error, but she was good at manoeuvring and, providing she kept her cool, there was no reason why she should touch the other car.

Her mind made up, she swung the steering-wheel hard over to the left and put her foot on the accelerator. She knew that the stranger couldn't possibly have anticipated her action. It had been much too sudden and impetuous. But, needing all her concentration on what she was doing, when only a hair's breadth now separated the sides of the two vehicles, she sensed rather than saw the blazing look he shot her.

Carefully she inched forward. She cast a glance in her wing-mirror and then breathed to Jet, 'I think we've made it!'

She spoke too soon. As she accelerated slightly to pull away she felt the back of her Peugeot touch the Jaguar. She swore, angry with herself for her ineptitude and with the other driver for his intransigence.

She drew up at the side of the track and got out. Since the Jaguar had been stationary, she was plainly liable for any damage to it.

She saw that the stranger was already examining the paintwork of his car. Hearing her shut her door, he straightened up and came towards her.

He was over six feet tall, dressed casually in a checked shirt and blue jeans that accentuated his rugged masculinity, revealing the breadth of his shoulders and the leanness of his hips.

Hair which was as straight as her own fell over his tanned forehead. It was black and in the sunshine had a bluish sheen like a raven's wing. The line of his jaw was strong, complementing his high cheekbones. Together with his other features, his hawkish brows and the slight dimple in his chin, it gave his face character.

The set of his mouth, which was sensual and yet stern, commanded her attention for an instant before her gaze rose to meet the unmistakable glitter of anger in his dark cobalt eyes. Electricity seemed to flicker along her nerves, throwing her momentarily off balance.

'Your little piece of exhibitionism didn't pay off, did it?' he began.

His sarcasm touched her on the raw.

'Why didn't you pull over when you saw me coming?' she demanded. 'Do you think you own the road?'

'If I'd known you were going to attempt such a crazy manoeuvre I'd have given you more room,' he fired back. His clipped tone revealed the tight hold he had over his temper. 'How long have you been driving?'

She knew what he was implying and, stung by his question, she retorted, 'Six years!'

'Which puts you at twenty-two, twenty-three?' His masculine gaze assessed her.

'I'm twenty-three,' she said coldly.

'A bit old to be driving like some reckless teenager let loose for the first time with Daddy's car,' he said.

She did not consider she had been reckless and his scathing observation made her spark with answering derision. 'And how old are you?'

'Is there a point to this question?' He frowned.

'Simply that thirty-something isn't the age to be driving like some arrogant rep let loose for the first time with a company car,' she retorted. 'If you'd acted like a gentleman I wouldn't have had to edge past you in the first place!'

She regretted her words the instant they were spoken. The stranger didn't look the kind of man to tolerate insolence from anyone, least of all from a red-haired sprite of a girl who barely reached his shoulder.

His dark brows came together, the glimmer of speculative amusement which flickered in his eyes taking her by surprise. She didn't show it, but she was relieved that with her attack she'd evoked not his anger but his sense of humour.

'Well, we all have to pay for our mistakes,' he said. 'Do you want to look at the damage?'

The Jaguar's gleaming paintwork made the score marks caused by the side of her bumper very visible. She licked the ball of her thumb and rubbed one of the scratches with it in the vain hope that it looked worse than it was. She wryly had to accept the fact that not even a good car wax would hide the marks.

'I . . . I've scratched your paintwork a little,' she admitted, straightening up.

'Perceptive of you,' he gibed. 'I suppose you are insured?'

'Of course I'm insured!' she said. 'I wouldn't be on the road if I——'

'Who with?' he cut her short.

'I don't want to lose my no-claims bonus,' she told him. 'I'll meet the bill myself.'

He took a Mont Blanc pen from his shirt pocket.

'Then I'll need to know your address,' he said.

'I live at Pencarreg Hall, Bryn Uchel.'

Something flickered across the chiselled planes of the man's face in response to her reply. As if he was adding the information to the sum total he had formed of her, his dark eyes made a leisurely appraisal of her. His look was audacious and sensual, making her catch her breath imperceptibly. It was almost as though she were up for auction and he was considering putting in a bid for her, she thought crossly.

'So you're Meredith Jones,' he said.

Quizzical surprise showed in her eyes. Not only did the stranger know her name, but he had given it the correct Welsh pronunciation with the accent on the middle syllable. She demanded, 'How do you know who I am? You're not a local.'

'I'm more local than you think.'

'Your accent's English,' she challenged.

'I'm from Cornwall,' he told her, adding, 'I'll be in touch about the bill. Perhaps you'd like to see the estimate before deciding definitely that you want to meet it yourself.'

'No doubt it will be steep,' she said with antagonism, certain he meant to fleece her.

'If it is, it may teach you to be less impetuous in future,' he said.

With that he opened his car door and ducked into his Jaguar, his dark hair gleaming in the sun. Annoyed with herself for staring after him as if he compelled her gaze, Meredith pivoted sharply and returned to her own car.

Deciding she had simmered over the incident long enough, she dismissed it from her mind as she turned in through the gates that led to the secluded country house that was her home. Pencarreg Hall, which had been bought by her grandfather at the beginning of the century, was set against one of the most beautiful mountain ranges in North Wales and dated back almost three hundred years.

Grey gables and tall chimneys punctuated the long steep roof, while mullioned windows looked out over an ornate stone balustrade to well-tended lawns and rose-gardens. Meredith parked on the gravel drive and with Jet at her heels went into the house through the elegant porch.

Her sister-in-law was in the drawing-room idly flicking through a glossy magazine. She was four years older than Meredith and every bit as striking to look at, though in a totally different way. Her beautiful blonde hair fell over her shoulder in a plait Rapunzel would have envied. One glance at her porcelain skin confirmed that its colour was completely natural.

She was wearing dark blue trousers and a pale blue top. The colour suited her, emphasising the startling blueness of her eyes. Soft-voiced and very poised, she radiated an aura of coolly balanced sex-appeal.

When she chose she could be lazily amusing and she made everyone laugh with her dry observations. On the whole Meredith got on well with her, and of late they'd become quite close friends.

'Hi,' she began, glancing up from her magazine. 'I was toying with the idea of joining you at the beach for a swim, but you're back earlier than I expected.'

'I thought I'd give Margred a hand,' Meredith explained, dropping into an armchair for a minute.

'There's loads of time yet,' Jessica said. Reaching for her cigarettes, she shook one out of the packet. 'Besides,' she went on, 'Margred can cook dinner for ten with her eyes shut.'

'I know she can,' Meredith agreed, 'but it's not fair to put on her.'

The remark wasn't meant to imply any criticism of her sister-in-law. Jessica was staying at the house as a guest. She naturally wasn't expected to help when they entertained.

'It should be an interesting evening,' Jessica remarked. She dropped the match she had used to light her cigarette into the ashtray. 'What do you think this whiz-kid from South Africa will be like?'

'I've no idea,' Meredith replied, and then amended her answer.

Her father, she remembered, had raged for days over the terms he had been forced to offer the mining engineer in order to persuade him to join the company.

'He must be tough to have driven such a hard bargain with Dad,' she said.

Jessica nodded, a pensive light in her blue eyes. 'Not many people get the better of Gerallt,' she agreed.

Meredith smiled at the accuracy of her sister-in-law's observation. 'If Rhys Treherne knows his job, he'll more than justify the salary he's being paid,' she commented. 'Dad was delighted with the geologists' report. He always said the gold-bearing lodes weren't worked out.'

The Mynydd y Glyn mines which were run by her father were hidden in the mountains above the glinting water and yellow sands of the estuary. In her grandfather's day they had yielded some sixty-four thousand ounces of the precious metal.

But for some years commercial extraction had ceased to be viable.

The gold, unlike that found in the major gold-producing area of the world, was scattered not in convenient veins, but in small pockets. These pockets were trapped in a quartz vein which criss-crossed through the mine's five miles of tunnels. Problems with drilling had forced the company to turn its attention to the extraction of other minerals and the old workings had been abandoned.

New advances in mining technology and the rarity value of Welsh gold, which carried a twenty per cent premium, had since altered the situation. Now a two-year exploration programme was going ahead and, needing an expert with experience of hard-rock mining, Meredith's father had enticed Rhys Treherne into the company as the technical director in charge of the project.

'I wonder if he's married,' Jessica said idly.

'He's here on his own as far as I know,' Meredith said.

Her well-defined dark brows came together as a thought suddenly struck her. Treherne was a Cornish name. Hadn't the hateful stranger whose car she had touched said he was from Cornwall?

'What is it?' Jessica enquired, reading her expression.

'I had a bit of an altercation with the driver of another car as I was coming back from the beach,' Meredith explained, golden sparks in her eyes. 'It suddenly occurred to me that perhaps... No,' she decided. 'It couldn't have been him.

What puzzled me was that the man knew who I was.'

'How intriguing!' Jessica exclaimed, entertained by the mystery. 'What makes you so sure he wasn't Rhys Treherne?'

'He didn't talk with a South African accent. He was English and very sarcastic.'

'I hope you gave as good as you got. Oh, before I forget,' Jessica announced, 'Trefor phoned a short while ago. He's going to be late this evening.'

The remark scarcely registered with Meredith. Her mind was still on the car accident, or rather on the man she deemed responsible for it. She pulled herself together. 'Did he say why?' she asked.

Jessica shook her head. 'He's making rather a habit of altering your plans at the last moment, isn't he?' she observed.

'He can't help it if there's an emergency.'

'He's hardly on call at the hospital every weekend,' Jessica pointed out.

'No, but he's rostered on in Casualty at the moment.'

'I think he's too sure of you,' Jessica gave her opinion.

Meredith was beginning to wonder herself. There was no doubt that part of her appeal initially had been the fact that she hadn't been easy to win, but, refusing to be drawn on the subject, she said, 'He won't be very late, I expect.'

She left Jessica to her magazine, and joined the housekeeper in the large practical kitchen. It had a homely feel, with a polished floor of Welsh slate and a low ceiling. It was the same age as the rest of the house, yet it was a remarkably easy kitchen to run. Pine base and wall units meant that everything was to hand and provided heaps of work space.

Margred was at the kitchen table, chopping mint.

'Have you come to raid the cake tin?' she said, glancing up with a smile.

Her joking question referred to when Meredith and her brother had been children.

'I could certainly eat a slice of your cherry cake,' Meredith laughed, 'but as it's not all that long till dinner I'll refrain. What can I do to help?'

'Let's see,' Margred mused. 'I've made a fruit salad for dessert. Can I leave it to you to make the trifle?'

'How about profiteroles instead?' Meredith suggested.

'Even better,' came the ready answer.

She chatted to the housekeeper while she made the choux pastry and piped out the pastry cases. She had filled them with cream and was pouring on the thick chocolate sauce when her father came into the kitchen on his way to the cellar to choose the wine.

A distinguished-looking man with bushy eyebrows and a craggy face, Gerallt Jones had been a widower for close on thirteen years. It had been after his wife's death and a series of unsatisfactory domestic arrangements that he had converted part of the house into a self-contained flat and advertised for a live-in housekeeper.

In no time the house had been running as smoothly as it had done when Meredith's mother had been alive. Margred was dependable and wonderfully efficient and Gerallt, who knew he could rely upon her to cope with any domestic crisis, treated her with a deference he showed few other people.

'Is that a leg of lamb I can smell cooking?' he asked with obvious approval.

'I thought I'd prepare something traditional,' Margred told him.

'How was your game of golf?' Meredith asked.

'Evan Hughes is getting hard to beat,' her father chuckled. 'That golfing holiday he had on the Algarve has really sharpened up his playing.'

'You ought to take a break, too, some time,' Meredith said. 'It would do you good.'

'It would bore me to death,' Gerallt answered, dismissing the suggestion.

'Probably,' Meredith was forced to agree. An affectionate smile touched her lips. 'Two days with nothing to do and you'd be hankering to get back to work again.'

Her father surveyed the silver tray that was piled high with cream-filled choux pastry cases.

'Profiteroles,' he observed. 'I suppose that means Trefor will be joining us again. You know, I think it's time I asked that young man what his intentions are.'

'Dad!' Meredith exclaimed in protest.

'Well,' her father demanded, his voice stern but not without humour, 'is he going to be my son-in-law or isn't he?'

Meredith's shoulders hunched in a tiny shrug that conveyed the impression that the thought of marrying Trefor had never even entered her head.

'I don't know,' she said.

Gerallt frowned slightly as he considered his very attractive and very independent daughter. 'From the time you turned sixteen there's always been some ardent admirer or another knocking at the door,' he stated.

Bright, beautiful and as graceful as a dancer, Meredith never made any effort to captivate, but captivate she invariably did. Yet until recently no thought of settling down had entered her head.

'When are you going to decide that one of them measures up?' her father continued.

'I think Trefor measures up nicely,' she answered.

'Hmm!' came the sceptical reply.

'We get on very well together,' Meredith insisted.

'There are men of thought and there are men of action. One day, if that mild-mannered medic you get on so well with doesn't wake up, he'll find out that someone else has stolen a march on him and whisked you off to the altar under his nose,' Gerallt predicted, a glimmer of a smile in his steely grey eyes.

Margred, who had been an amused onlooker during the exchange, remarked laughingly after he had disappeared down the steps into the cellar, 'It's a good job you know your own mind. If you didn't your father would bulldoze you into marriage.'

'Dad wants grandchildren,' Meredith said, and tried not to feel guilty that at twenty-three she was still single. 'Stephen's death hit him very hard. If he had a grandson he'd feel there was someone to carry on from him at the mine.'

A look of sympathy flickered across the housekeeper's face. She was fully aware of the blow it had been to Meredith to lose her only brother.

'Stephen's death hit us all very hard,' she answered quietly.

'You're right,' Meredith said, her throat tight. It was a painful subject and, not wanting the ache of grief to well up keenly, she asked, changing the subject, 'Is there anything else I can do, Margred?'

'No, that's fine,' the housekeeper assured her.

'Then I'll go and get changed.'

Gerallt was at the front door greeting the Hugheses when she came downstairs half an hour later wearing a flattering dress with dropped shoulder seams, bracelet-length sleeves and a full, graceful skirt.

'Are we the first to arrive?' Elen's voice floated into the hall from the porch. 'I'm afraid we usually are,' she laughed.

'Someone has to be first, so why not us?' her husband quipped.

'Of course you're not too early,' Gerallt insisted. 'Come on in.'

'Hello, Meredith.' Elen smiled as she came into the hall. 'What a pretty dress! Green is really your colour.'

The drawing-room was full of talk and laughter and Meredith was circulating with a tray of cocktail snacks when the doorbell rang again.

'That will be Trefor, I imagine,' she said to Jessica as she handed her the tray.

Her heels tapping on the polished wood-block floor, she went into the hall. She opened the front door wide. A tall dark-haired man stood outside and, recognising him, Meredith felt her heart give a jolt of dismay.

He was extremely well dressed in a charcoal-grey suit that enhanced his strong, lean build, and the physical impact he made on her was the same as when she had first met him that afternoon when he had been wearing jeans and a checked shirt. Her smile of welcome promptly vanished as she stared into the man's strikingly masculine face.

Her reaction seemed to amuse him.

'Hello, Meredith,' he began.

She couldn't understand why the sound of her name on his lips should antagonise her, but it did.

'I had an ominous feeling you'd turn out to be Rhys Treherne,' she said.

CHAPTER TWO

'So you finally got round to putting two and two together,' Rhys mocked.

'It would have helped if instead of pretending, rather childishly, to be from Cornwall, you'd told me you were South African,' Meredith pointed out coolly, her chin tilting as she looked up at him.

For a Celt she was tall, and few men towered above her as Rhys did. His dark suit emphasised his strong dark looks. She didn't particularly admire his choice of tie, polka-dots on maroon silk, but she had to admit that his immaculate and urbane appearance was arresting.

'Wrong again,' he gibed. 'I am from Cornwall. I happen to have worked for the last two years in Johannesburg.'

'I think you'll find gold-mining in North Wales very different from gold-mining on the Rand,' she told him, as she stood back to allow him over the threshold.

'But not so different from tin-mining in Cornwall,' he answered.

'I'm afraid I fail to see the similarity between tin and gold,' she said.

'The similarity is in the mining methods,' he answered, as they crossed the hall together. 'It seems you don't take much interest in your father's company or you'd have known that.'

The implied criticism annoyed her. Veiled sparks coming into her amber eyes, she retorted, 'Despite your very obvious assumption, Mr Treherne, I am not some silly spoiled ignoramus.'

'My, aren't we quick to take offence!' he mocked.

She felt her temper rise. 'And you're very quick to criticise when you know nothing about me!' she returned.

'We could alter that,' he suggested.

The line of his mouth was firm, but there was an amused glitter in his dark eyes.

'First we'd have to want to,' she replied pointedly.

'Our brush on the highway got us off to a bad start,' Rhys said as, taking hold of her by the arm, he refused to allow her to sweep ahead of him into the drawing-room.

'Yes,' she agreed. 'It did.'

'You acted stupidly and impulsively this afternoon,' he told her.

She glared at him and then, battling with herself, she dropped her gaze as the honesty at the core of her nature forced her to concede she had been in the wrong. It was possible that although Rhys hadn't backed up he would have pulled in at the side of the road to give her more room if she hadn't been so hasty.

'All right, I'm sorry,' she said, unable to help the fact that she didn't sound it.

'Apology accepted,' Rhys drawled. 'You said that very prettily.'

He was making fun of her! She had a lively sense of humour and she wasn't a person who couldn't take a joke against herself, but she wasn't used to being laughed at.

Instinct told her that if she rose to his remark, as she was sorely tempted to do, she would amuse him even more. She decided to let him think his mockery had glanced off her.

'I do most things prettily.'

'I don't doubt it.'

As he spoke his gaze made a leisurely appraisal of her, the lazy intimacy of his eyes lending an innuendo to his reply. It was as if he was mentally undressing her while considering what she would be like in bed—his bed!

For an instant she stared back at him, a flush of heat enveloping her. The very air seemed to tingle and, in a flurry of uncharacteristic confusion, she took a step in the direction of the drawing-room. The wood-block floor was highly polished and she skidded a little. A capable hand shot out.

'Careful!' Rhys said as he steadied her.

'Th... thank you.' She sounded breathless.

'You seem to be accident prone,' Rhys chuckled.

'I obviously need someone like you around to look after me,' she replied, her quick wit returning for all she felt so flustered.

Rhys's smile was attractive and she was aware that in response to it her heart gave a strange little kick against her ribs.

'Maybe you do, at that,' he agreed mockingly. 'Did I bruise you?' he asked.

'You have a strong grip.' She evaded the question and stopped rubbing her arm, though she still felt the imprint of his touch, firm and vaguely disturbing. 'Come on in and meet Dad's friends.'

She led the way into the drawing-room, very aware that his footfall, close on her heels, was as soft and as sure as a hunter's. Her father immediately stood up and came towards them.

'Rhys, good to see you!' he began. 'I expect Meredith's already introduced herself?'

'With great aplomb,' he said.

The glint in his eyes as his dark gaze flickered to hers told her he had been amused by the hint of hauteur with which she had informed him of her address that afternoon.

'I'm glad I made an impact,' she murmured sweetly.

Unaware of the hidden barb in her reply, Gerallt remarked with satisfaction, 'It's good the two of you seem to have hit it off so well. Now, let's see, who else don't you know here?'

While her father made the introductions, Meredith returned to her seat on the sofa and resumed a conversation with Elen. Outwardly she was serene; inwardly she felt uncharacteristically ruffled.

No man had ever looked her over as Rhys Treherne had done in the hall, as though she was his for the taking. The fact that for an instant or two he'd completely shattered her cool poise added fuel to the fire of her indignant resentment. Her first assessment of him had been correct. He was arrogant and presumptuous!

With several conversations going on at the same time in the room, she was able to ignore him without it appearing pointed to anyone else present. Not that he needed any special attention from her as hostess. Sharp-witted, indomitable and urbane, he was a good mixer. Even Jessica, who often seemed rather remote, was sparkling, she noticed, in his company.

It was some while later that her gaze inadvertently collided with his. He was seated across the room from her, chatting to the doctor and his wife and being rather charming to Jackie, their very nice but somewhat nondescript daughter. Beyond him was the grandfather clock, which Meredith, anxious in her role as hostess, had looked at not five minutes before.

She glanced away as he quirked a dark eyebrow in her direction, questioning her preoccupation with the time. Damn him, she thought irritably, did he miss nothing?

Dinner was ready and she was on tenterhooks listening for the sound of Trefor's car. Her father, who disliked keeping his guests waiting, had already subjected her to several glowering looks.

Wondering whatever was keeping her boyfriend, she left the room to give him a call. She used the phone in the study to dial his number. Her fingers toyed with the cord as she waited for him to answer, but the phone continued to ring.

Relieved, she decided he must be about to knock at the front door at any moment. She was on the point of ringing off when Trefor picked up the receiver.

'Trefor, I hoped you'd be on your way by now!' she began in concern. 'We're all ready to have dinner and Dad's about to explode.'

'Darling, I'm sorry. I've only just this minute got in. I've been to Oxford. There's a contraflow system on the motorway and the traffic was diabolical.'

'What were you doing in Oxford?' she asked, surprised.

'I had lunch there,' he told her.

'It's a long way to drive for lunch,' she said, rather put out with him.

'You're telling me,' he said. 'Someone I used to work with invited me. I went only because I was pressed into it. When I realised I'd be late back I gave you a ring.'

'Jessica gave me the message,' she answered.

'I tried to phone you again from Welshpool but the damn call-box wasn't working,' Trefor told her. 'I'm afraid you'd better count me out for this evening. There's no way I can drive over to your place in under half an hour, and I haven't even changed yet. I'll make it up to you to-morrow, darling. Forgive me for letting you down like this?'

The sincere note in his voice coaxed a wan smile out of her.

'OK, I'll forgive you this time,' she said. 'But don't let me down next Saturday.'

It was a teasing warning rather than a plea.

'I haven't forgotten,' Trefor laughed. 'We've been asked to a housewarming party. I'll be there, I promise.'

He would have chatted longer but, mindful of her father's guests, Meredith brought the call to an end.

'I must go, Trefor,' she said. 'I'll see you tomorrow.'

She removed his place setting from the table and then went to tell the housekeeper that there was no need to hold the meal back any longer.

The dinner, despite the hiccup in timing, went off perfectly. Meredith sat at one end of the table while her father sat at the other. Rhys Treherne was placed on her right, so that she was obliged to talk to him.

She hadn't taken to him, but she had to concede he was an interesting conversationalist, and very well informed. Several times during the course of the evening she found herself chatting to him about current affairs and about his job.

'Where else have you worked apart from South Africa?' she asked.

'I spent a year or so in Canada working for one of the large mining companies out there,' he told her. 'I thought I might decide to settle in Quebec, but then the job in South Africa came up.'

'You're not the sort of person who puts down roots, then,' she commented.

'I haven't to date, but perhaps it's time I did,' he said. 'You seem to have thrived on staying in one place.'

Was he teasing her? She didn't know him well enough to tell, nor could she work out why her pulse seemed to flutter each time her eyes came into contact with his.

'Which part of Cornwall are you from?' she asked, changing the topic.

The slight quirk of his mouth told her he'd guessed she preferred talking about him to talking about herself.

'I own two cottages in Trelick, near Redruth.' He took a sip of wine. There was something about his every action that was inherently and arrogantly masculine, she thought, diverted for a moment from what he was saying. 'My stepfather lives in one of them.'

'And the other?' she asked.

'It's rented out as holiday accommodation at the moment,' he told her. 'I decided against selling it when I went abroad.'

'I suppose now you've bought Glan-wern you'll put it on the market,' she said.

A speculative dark brow quirked at her. 'News gets around,' he commented.

'In a small place it always does,' she answered. 'But, in this case, Dad happened to mention you'd bought Glan-wern.'

'It's a fine house,' Rhys said, 'but I'll still hang on to my other place. The price of property only ever goes one way.'

'You sound like a property speculator,' she remarked.

'And you sound as if you disapprove,' he returned.

'I'm not against second homes,' she told him. 'I just think it's a shame when young people have to move away from the villages where they were born because outsiders push the house prices up. It's something that's happening more and more.'

'Luckily we've had no houses burnt down

here,' Jackie ventured shyly as she caught the end of what Meredith was saying. 'Your house should be quite safe, Rhys.'

'I'm insured for fire,' he answered, a glimmer of a smile in his dark eyes.

The subject of arson attacks brought Evan Hughes and the doctor into the conversation. Empty cottages had been at risk for several years from arson attacks by a group of extremists who resented the English buying property in North Wales.

'The problem's blown up all out of proportion by the media,' Hughes said. 'One cottage is set fire to and it hits the headlines in the national newspapers, making everyone think that houses are being burned down in Wales left, right and centre.'

'And that of course is exactly what the extremists want the English to think,' the doctor said. 'If I was buying a holiday home here I'd choose a place in the town, and I might see that there was someone to keep an eye on it occasionally, but that would be the only precaution I'd take.'

'It's the outlying houses that are the most at risk,' Meredith agreed, adding, as she glanced at Rhys, 'Glan-wern would make an ideal target.'

'I hope you're not thinking of setting fire to it,' he mocked, picking her up on her choice of words.

His inflexion needled her. She had been flawlessly polite to him at dinner, yet it seemed he sensed she didn't care for him. As the others laughed at his quip she replied, 'I was warning you to be careful.'

'I'm touched by your concern,' he said.

She doubted that any of the others realised he was ribbing her, he sounded so sincere. Deciding to rib him back in the same way, she smiled, meaning the exact opposite of what she was saying.

'I can't help hoping you're going to put down those roots you were talking about here.'

The set of Rhys's mouth was suspiciously firm and, coupled with the amused glitter in his eyes, it told her that, even though his reaction wasn't what she would have wished, he had certainly caught her meaning.

'How do you like Bryn Uchel?' Jackie asked, blushing a little as she spoke.

It was plain from the blush that her friend was obviously not impervious to Rhys's charisma. He treated her question with a deferential charm that Meredith had to concede was attractive. It raised the question of why he didn't treat her in the same manner.

Hearing her name spoken at the other end of the table, she glanced up.

'I was saying that the praise for the profiteroles goes to you,' Gerallt relayed Elen's compliment to her.

'Besides being an excellent cook, what else do you do?' Rhys asked as the meal came to an end.

'I teach music at the local school,' she answered.

'When I saw the grand piano in the drawing-room I wondered who played it,' he said. 'Do you play just the one instrument?'

'No, I play several. I give lessons on the saxophone and on the guitar.'

'What about piano lessons?' Rhys asked.

'Yes, I give those as well,' she said.

'Just at school or here at the house?'

'Why? Are you thinking of brushing up your technique?' she asked innocently and had to smile inwardly.

She'd been just longing for a chance to score a point against him and he'd hit the ball right into her court.

'I was thinking more along the lines of trying a duet with you,' Rhys said, a glint in his eyes. The more she sparred with him, and somehow it seemed she couldn't help herself, the more diverting he seemed to find her. 'Looking at your hands, I'm sure you have an excellent touch.'

Was it her imagination or was there a slight sexual overtone in his mocking remark?

'A good ear is every bit as important as a fine touch,' she said rather coolly.

'Do you always drop the temperature to zero when you think a man's making a pass at you?' Rhys enquired with lazy humour.

His charisma was such that she *had* thought he was making a pass at her, and now she felt utterly ridiculous.

'I'm not so conceited,' she said, blushing, 'that I think every man who sits next to me at the dinner table is flirting with me.'

'Then you must have found a lot of dinner parties very dull,' Rhys answered. 'There's a lot to be said for the gentle art of flirting. At any rate it beats long after-dinner speeches.'

His teasing comment struck a chord and, in spite of herself, laughter came into her eyes.

'They can be rather tedious,' she agreed.

'Then you'll be glad to know I keep mine short and to the point,' he quipped.

It crossed her mind that such was his magnetism that he would command the attention of his audience no matter how long he spoke for and, as it did so, the realisation struck her that talking to him she was neglecting the rest of her father's guests.

'I think we're ready for coffee,' she said. 'If you'll excuse me I'll go and tell Margred.'

The dinner party was late breaking up. Meredith's father was a convivial host and it was well after midnight before the doctor's wife patted her husband on the arm and said, 'We ought to be making a move.'

'What, already?'

'What do you mean, already?' his wife smiled. 'Look at the time!'

'Good heavens, I hadn't realised it was so late,' he laughed.

Elen and Evan stayed a little longer and then, they, too, said they must be going. While Gerallt stood chatting with them in the front porch, Rhys joined Meredith, who had said her goodbyes in the hall.

'It's been a very pleasant evening,' he drawled.

'I'm glad you've enjoyed it,' she murmured politely.

The masculine line of Rhys's mouth quirked at her answer.

'You know, if I hadn't met you earlier today I'd have no idea that you've a redhead's temper. Who were you angry or upset with that you opted to clash with me?'

His astute question took her by surprise.

'No one,' she said, denying that Trefor had anything to do with her accidentally scratching Rhys's Jaguar. 'I've said I'll pay for the damage. Can we now leave the subject alone?'

'Why not, since we've plenty of other things to talk about?'

'Such as?' she asked.

'You, and what I'm supposed to make of you.'

'Why should you want to fathom me?' she asked, her chin tilting.

'Because you're unpredictable, and I like that in a woman,' Rhys told her.

'I'm flattered you've found something to like at last.' She was certain he thought her spoilt and headstrong, and her tone was ironic.

Rhys's smile was amused.

'There's a lot I like,' he returned. 'Goodnight, Meredith.'

She was not sure what she should make of his comment, and her gaze followed him as he went through into the porch to say goodbye to her father. The light in the hall gleamed on the raven thickness of his hair. Masculine authority was stamped into every inch of him, commanding her attention for an instant.

Then, realising that once again she was staring after him, she returned to the drawing-room. Her sister-in-law had kicked off her smart court shoes now that all the guests had gone and was curled up on the sofa, enjoying a last liqueur.

'What happened to Trefor this evening?' she enquired lazily.

'He was out all day and got back too late to come over,' Meredith explained.

'I don't think anyone missed him, unless you did,' Jessica said, patting a yawn. 'I'm not knocking him, you understand, but Rhys is much better company.'

'Not in my book, he isn't,' Meredith felt obliged to say out of loyalty to Trefor, who respected her and made her feel safe. In contrast Rhys made her feel challenged in a way she couldn't quite analyse. 'Though I noticed Jackie seemed very taken with him,' she went on.

'That little mouse!' her sister-in-law said with a contemptuous laugh.

'That's unkind!' Meredith protested at once.

'She is a mouse,' Jessica insisted. She stretched, arching her supple back. 'I can tell you now, if she's after Rhys she's wasting her time. She's not his type.'

'Who would you say is?' Meredith asked, interested in spite of herself.

'Someone with both looks and intelligence,' Jessica replied. 'In other words, someone like you, or me.'

It was a statement Meredith found herself pondering on later as she got ready for bed. She believed she had a good sixth sense where men were concerned. That sense told her that Rhys would never fall under her spell, for the simple reason that he found her amusing.

Not that she cared. He had an aura of danger which she supposed a lot of women would find attractive, but he definitely wasn't the sort of man she would wish to be emotionally entangled with.

She twisted her head about as she unpinned her glossy hair, letting it cascade like a skein of silk about her shoulders. Quite possibly Jackie was already in love with him. If so she felt sorry for her.

She classed Rhys as a womaniser, someone who could be ruthless in a relationship. She had to concede that he was charismatic, albeit in a hard sort of way. He struck her, too, as the kind of man to be relied on in a crisis. But, even so, he wasn't the sort of man she would ever want as a lover, or a husband. Already it was clear to her, if not to him, that the most they could ever hope for was a very cool sort of friendship.

CHAPTER THREE

THE gaunt peaks that towered on either side of the mountain road were sharply etched against the sky. Summer clouds, drifting slowly, cast moving shadows over the massive shoulders of the mountains, dappling them in shades of dark green which made the sunlit slopes look all the more brilliant. Up on the high pastures sheep were grazing, insignificant dots against the grandeur of the landscape.

The sun-roof of Trefor's car was open and the breeze ruffled Meredith's hair as they drove along. As always the roads were quiet on a Sunday and on this particular stretch there wasn't another car in sight.

'Aren't Sundays peaceful?' she remarked.

'Hmm?' he said, slanting an enquiring glance at her.

'I hope you're attending to the road, if you're not attending to me,' she said, pulling his leg.

'I'm sorry,' he said with a rueful laugh, 'I was thinking of other things. What were you saying?'

In his late twenties, strong-jawed, with honest grey eyes and brown hair that was inclined to wave, Trefor was as affable as he looked. His equanimity was in striking contrast with Meredith's fire and sparkle.

They pulled up outside the wide frontage of the hotel where they often had lunch on a Sunday.

The dining-room, which was full of sunlight, overlooked the estuary, and the friendly and solicitous service made for a relaxing atmosphere.

'Will you start with the avocado salad as usual?' Trefor asked.

'No, I think I'll try something different today,' she said, deciding as she considered the menu, 'I'll have the toasted *brioche* with wild mushrooms.'

'My word, you are being quixotic!' Trefor laughed.

His teasing conjured up in her mind a hard masculine face.

'Do you think so?' she said, and then asked, 'Do you find me unpredictable?'

'Not usually, no,' he replied. 'You're impulsive, but that's not the same as being unpredictable. Why do you ask?'

'Dad's new fellow director called me unpredictable last night,' she explained.

'Maybe he meant it as a compliment,' Trefor suggested.

'Somehow I don't think so,' she replied.

'And do you care what he thinks of you?'

'No, not in the least,' she assured him.

'What's he like?'

'You mean Rhys?' she said. Compared to her boyfriend he wasn't handsome. There was too much hardness in his features, but there was an animal fierceness about him that was impressive, she had to admit. And yet he rubbed her up the wrong way. Why was it, she wondered, when others appeared to get along with him so easily? 'He certainly scored a hit with Jessica,' she commented, thinking of the way her sister-in-law had reacted to him. 'You know how distant she can be at times. Well, on Saturday she was completely different. She laughed and joked with Rhys as if she'd known him for ages.'

'I'm not asking you what Jessica thinks of him,' Trefor asked. 'I'm asking what do you think of him.'

'He's very sure of himself,' Meredith gave her judgement.

'Will he make a success of the exploration programme, do you think?' Trefor asked.

'Dad's sure of it.'

'But you'll wait and see,' her boyfriend guessed.

'No,' she said, realising that, though she had reservations about the man, she shared her father's confidence in him. 'I think he'll be good for the company.'

'I'm still surprised you didn't decide to work in it yourself,' Trefor commented. 'You can't say you're not interested in the business world.'

'I am,' she agreed. 'And I've always been interested in what goes on at the mine, but music's my first love.'

'I hoped I was,' he joked.

'You know what I mean,' she laughed and found herself thinking fleetingly that had she gone into the company she'd have found she was working alongside Rhys and no doubt sparring with him. She realised he disturbed her vaguely and, resolving to put him out of her mind, she said, changing the topic, 'Did I tell you I'm giving piano lessons at the house after school now?'

'You've always said you were too busy before,' Trefor replied.

'I know,' she agreed, 'but I kept being asked about private tuition and I felt mean saying no.'

'What does your father think of the idea?' he asked, quirking an amused eyebrow at her.

'He's a bit bemused by it,' Meredith admitted with a smile, 'but then I don't think he ever expected me to want a career.'

Since she had her own income from money left in trust to her by her mother, there was no need for Meredith to work at all. It was something she chose to do and enjoyed.

'Dad's a dear,' she went on, affectionate humour in her voice, 'but he hasn't caught up yet with modern ideas where women are concerned. He'd think nothing of it at all if I decided I wanted to stay home all day and be a lady of leisure.'

'Which is what your sister-in-law seems to have become,' Trefor said drily.

'That's not fair,' Meredith protested, coming swiftly to Jessica's defence.

'She gave up her job with your father's company in January and she hasn't done a day's work since,' he pointed out. A shadow flickered across Meredith's face and, seeing it, he reached out and took her hand. 'I'm sorry,' he said gently. 'I didn't mean to remind you.'

Meredith's brother and his wife had taken a skiing holiday in Switzerland that January. They'd been driving home to Bryn Uchel from the airport when they'd been involved in a head-on collision with another car.

Jessica had miraculously escaped from the accident with only minor injuries, but Stephen had been seriously hurt. He'd died two days later in hospital without ever regaining consciousness.

Jessica had seemed numbed by his death. She'd collapsed on the day of the funeral, and Gerallt and Meredith, afraid she was heading for a breakdown, had insisted that she come to stay at Pencarreg Hall for a while. These days she was far more her old self again, but she showed no sign of wanting to move back alone into the house she'd shared with Stephen.

'Jessica doesn't always show her feelings, but she's still very cut up,' Meredith said. 'She needs time to adjust to the accident. When she does eventually come to terms with it I'm sure she'll want to go back to work.'

He considered her, a musing light in his eyes. 'You're very loyal,' he said.

'And you're very hard on Jessica,' she replied.

It seemed he was about to reply, but changed his mind and signalled to the waiter for their bill.

There was an antiques fair being held at the hotel and as they crossed the foyer Meredith suggested they look in on it. She found it fascinating wandering round the various stalls. Interested in different things, she and Trefor separated for a while, meeting up by the exit when they'd browsed long enough.

The sun was still warm, though the shadows were beginning to lengthen, by the time they arrivéd back at her home. Trefor accepted her invitation to stay for dinner, but said he must be going shortly afterwards as he had to be at the hospital early the next morning.

Meredith saw him out and they were talking in the hall when he said with a bantering smile, 'Before I go we've got a guessing game to play.' He felt in his pocket and then swiftly put both hands behind his back.

'What are you hiding?' she asked, laughter in her eyes.

'Guess which hand,' he ordered. 'Left or right?'

Entering into the spirit of the game, she deliberated a moment and then decided, 'Left.'

'Left it is,' he told her, bringing his hand out from behind his back. 'Here, this is yours.'

She managed to feign pleasure as she saw the bracelet he held out to her. It was a wide band made of brass, heavily chased, and she had last seen it at the antiques fair where she had thought what a Victorian monstrosity it was.

'Oh, Trefor! You bought it for me! You shouldn't have!' she said.

'Surprised?' he smiled.

'Yes. I'd no idea!'

'I bought it for you while you were looking at the Royal Doulton china,' Trefor told her. 'It's only brass, of course...'

'It's lovely,' she insisted quickly, afraid he had sensed her delight wasn't genuine.

He fastened the bracelet on her wrist before kissing her palm. 'Because of work, I've neglected you a bit of late,' he said. 'That's to make up for it.'

She closed the front door as his car disappeared down the drive. Then she went back into the hall. She was right by the phone on the hall table when it started ringing.

She picked up the receiver to hear a male voice ask, 'Is that Meredith?'

A curious prickling stirred at the back of her neck and automatically her hand went to erase the sensation. She was sure she knew the voice.

'Speaking,' she answered.

'It's Rhys Treherne.'

'I'll call Dad for you,' she said politely.

For no reason at all her pulse had quickened, a reflex response to the forceful personality at the other end of the line.

'It wasn't your father I wanted to speak to,' Rhys told her.

'Oh?' she questioned, adding, as she worked out the answer herself, 'Then you must want Jessica.'

'Try again,' he suggested mockingly.

'You . . . called to talk to me,' she deduced, obviously puzzled.

Rhys couldn't have had the repair work done to his car already, not on a Sunday.

'I was wondering if you'd like to have dinner with me Wednesday night?' he said smoothly.

Her heart gave a jolt of surprise. She was used to men finding her attractive, but she'd no idea she'd caught the masculine attention of Rhys Treherne. He'd been far too mocking!

'I'm afraid I'm going out that evening,' she replied.

'How about Thursday, then?' he asked.

'I can't manage Thursday either,' she said.

'That leaves Friday.'

'I'm busy then, too,' she said. 'I'm seeing my boyfriend.'

'So you're playing hard to get,' Rhys drawled.

For an instant she stared at the receiver, astounded by the matchless arrogance of the man. With a quick flash of temper she told him, 'I'm not playing at anything, Mr Treherne. I *am* hard to get!'

'I'll remember that,' came the mockingly amused reply.

The line clicked as he rang off. Cross that she'd been too slow to come back with a rejoinder, she banged down the receiver.

'Who was that on the phone?' Jessica enquired as she came into the hall a few moments later.

A trace of irritation lingering in her voice, Meredith answered, 'Rhys Treherne.'

Something flickered for an instant in the depths of Jessica's blue eyes.

'Well, well!' she said with a soft laugh. 'I take my hat off to the man! He's a fast worker. I didn't think he'd call you quite so soon.'

'What made you think he'd ring me at all?' Meredith demanded.

'I could tell, watching him last night, that he was interested in you,' Jessica explained with a languid shrug. 'Did he ask you for a date?'

Meredith nodded.

'And?'

'I told him I was busy.'

'You turned him down, you mean?' Jessica said. 'Well, I don't imagine that happens very often.'

Meredith didn't doubt it. Rhys's arrogance suggested that he was used to taking his pick where women were concerned. Successful, dynamic and darkly good-looking, he'd probably broken a good many hearts. But hers was not to be numbered among them. She had too strong an instinct for self-preservation to risk getting involved with a man who, if her instincts were correct, was hard, sardonic and predatory.

The week seemed to fly and she came home from school on Friday in a buoyant weekend mood. She was later than usual, having stayed on to fit in another rehearsal for the school concert. It was coming together well, and she hummed a snatch of one of the tunes from it.

The evening was warm and sunny and she was on her way to the kitchen in search of an iced drink when the housekeeper came into the hall.

'You've only just missed Trefor,' she began. 'He rang about five minutes ago to say he won't be able to see you tomorrow.'

'I'll call him back,' she said, bewildered by his behaviour. He claimed he was in love with her, but lately he'd done nothing but alter their plans.

'He'll be in Theatre now,' Margred told her. 'He said he'd give you a ring later.'

'I see,' Meredith said, her voice a shade clipped. 'Thanks, Margred.'

But she didn't see, she didn't see at all. She was trying to put a brave face on it while resentment rippled through her. Why was Trefor treating her in this cavalier way?

She fully expected her boyfriend to phone her when he came off duty to explain. When after dinner she still hadn't heard from him she tried his number, but there was no answer and, cross with him, she went into the drawing-room.

She sat down at the piano and began to play one of Chopin's *études*. The study was tranquil, unlike her amber eyes, which mirrored her thoughts. She was always understanding when Trefor had to cancel their plans because of his work, but was she too understanding? He'd given her his word that he wouldn't let her down for the party!

Giving rein to her anger, she shattered the oasis of melodic calm. Four impassioned chords launched into a fierce turbulent study that required both force and control. Her quick fingers flew over the keyboard, producing a torrential cascade of music that gave expression to her emotions.

The first she knew of her audience of one was when she heard a round of applause. Startled, she glanced up to see Rhys Treherne standing in the doorway.

As ever, the impact he made on her was in direct relation to the aura of virility he exuded. He was wearing a navy business suit. The jacket, which was a perfect fit across his powerful shoulders, was open, showing an immaculate white shirt that contrasted with his tan. A navy and indigo silk tie matched the darkness of his eyes.

'Bravo,' he said, obviously impressed by her playing.

'Thank you,' she managed, hoping he hadn't realised she'd been taking her temper out on the music.

A black eyebrow rose a fraction of an inch. 'Is that a blush?' he mocked gently.

It was, but she didn't appreciate his commenting on it. The truth was, his masculine presence unsettled her.

Ignoring his question, she said, 'How long have you been standing there?'

'Long enough to appreciate your rendering of Chopin. Do you always play with such feeling and intensity?'

'Chopin's supposed to be played with feeling,' she told him. 'Who let you in?'

'I haven't walked in to steal the family silver,' he assured her.

'That wasn't what I meant,' she insisted.

He didn't contradict her statement. It was his chuckle that said he knew full well what she meant and was amused by her.

'Your housekeeper opened the front door to me,' he said. 'I had a business meeting in Cardiff today. I dropped by to let your father know the outcome of it.'

'It went well, I imagine,' she commented.

'As it happens,' he agreed. 'Was that a lucky guess on your part?'

'Not exactly. You have a reputation for being a very hard man to get the better of in a business deal.' She stood up from the piano stool and indicated one of the armchairs to him. 'Dad's out at the moment, but he should be back shortly. Would you like coffee?' she asked with cool good manners.

'No, thanks. Entertain me instead by playing that *étude* again.'

The tilt of her chin was defiant. In a prickly mood she said, 'Is that an order or a request?'

'It's a request,' he mocked. 'I get the impression you don't take orders.'

'Any more than you do!'

A hard smile curved the line of his mouth. 'Are you suggesting we're two of a kind?'

She tossed her head back. 'It might explain why we seem to strike sparks off each other,' she gibed.

'It might indeed,' he murmured, his dark gaze holding hers.

As she stared back into their cobalt depths she found it hard to catch her breath for an instant without knowing why.

'Do you want me to turn the music for you?' he prompted.

'I know the *étude* by heart,' she said, recovering herself swiftly, unaware that her very coolness was a dare to any man's virility.

Her technique was faultless as she played the piece once more. When she glanced up from the final chord Rhys was watching her, his head tilted in an attitude of masculine appraisal.

'You gave the piece far more fire and passion when you didn't know anyone was listening,' he said. 'It seems I inhibit you.'

He was taunting her, she was certain of it from the glint in his eyes. Her mouth tightened a little.

She was not going to emerge from this tilt the loser.

'You might be a maestro for all I know,' she said. 'If I didn't give the piece as much feeling as before it was because I was waiting for you to find fault with my playing.'

'Then let me put your mind at rest,' he replied. 'I don't even read music.'

'In which case, how were you going to turn the pages for me?' she was quick to demand.

'With difficulty!'

His answer was so unexpected that she burst out laughing. It was an engaging sound, a sound that was as pleasing to listen to as she was to look at.

'I thought perhaps you had a sense of humour,' Rhys gibed gently.

She was quick to retaliate in kind. 'I have a good sense of humour when I'm not being laughed at.'

'You mean you like men to take you seriously.' A hint of a smile softened his mouth.

'Most men do take me seriously,' she told him.

'I can imagine,' he drawled. 'Especially if you look at them the way you're looking at me.'

Candour and surprise flashed into her amber eyes. Too sharp to miss their fleeting expression, Rhys said, 'Are you telling me you don't *know*?'

'Know what?' she said. 'You've lost me.'

'It seems I have,' he agreed.

She gave him a questioning look. Then when he didn't explain she said, her manner friendlier now that he'd made her laugh, 'Would you like a drink while you're waiting?'

'Thanks, I'll have a Scotch.'

As he spoke, Jet nosed round the door and came padding into the drawing-room. Despite a pugnacious appearance and a ferocious-sounding bark, he was the gentlest of dogs, just as he was one of the ugliest. He went up to Rhys, tail wagging.

'Neat or with water?' she asked, crossing over to the drinks' cabinet.

'Neat,' he told her, patting Jet. 'Is this the family's dog, or is he yours?'

She glanced over her shoulder. The way he was scratching Jet's head told her that he liked animals. Unconsciously she cemented the rapport that was building between them by joking, 'Yes, Jet's mine, so no cracks please about dogs resembling their owners.'

Amusement played across the hard planes of Rhys's face. 'Are you fishing for compliments?' he quipped.

'And if I were?' Her question was playful.

'I'd tell you that your dog has very intelligent eyes.'

Laughter kindled in her own. The same electricity that made sparks quick to fly when they were together also made for a quick play of wit between them. She poured a Scotch for him and a glass of Curaçao for herself while he strolled over to examine the miner's lamp that was displayed on the bureau to the left of the fireplace.

'Do you keep this in the house for luck?'

'Not really. It was my grandfather's,' she told him.

He picked it up and read aloud the lettering that was stamped on the brass base.

'*Mynydd y Glyn mwynglawdd.*'

His pronunciation was perfect.

'With an accent like that you'll soon pass for a native,' she teased. He smiled and, referring to the lamp, she went on, 'My grandfather was quite a character by all accounts. He always said he didn't need a geologist to tell him where to drill. He claimed he could smell gold.'

'Some people can,' Rhys said.

'I understand you're one of them,' she replied. 'Apparently Grandfather's partner was too.'

'I thought your grandfather owned the mine outright?' Rhys questioned.

'No, he owned it jointly with a man called Tudor Morgan,' she answered. 'Then, round about 1945, my grandfather had a heart attack and was forced to retire. Dad was already working in the company by then, and when eventually Mr Morgan retired as well he sold his share of the business to my father.'

'He had no son to carry on from him, I take it,' Rhys guessed.

'Just a daughter, and she eloped when she was in her teens with a much older man,' Meredith said. 'Father and daughter weren't on speaking terms after that.'

'What was his daughter's name?' he asked.

She wrinkled her forehead as she thought. 'I can't remember,' she said. 'Dad would, though. All I know is that Mr Morgan was furious about the marriage. Apparently he'd been dead set against the match from the word go.'

'Because of the age-gap?' Rhys asked, taking a sip of whisky.

'I'm not sure,' she admitted, adding, 'I think it must have been more than that, because he cut her out of his will. The rift between them was never healed. She didn't even come back home when he was dying.'

'Perhaps she didn't know her father was ill,' Rhys suggested. His dark brows were drawn together, adding to the look of strength in his face.

'Perhaps,' she agreed, pondering on the story, 'but it was sad just the same. You'd have thought, wouldn't you, that before he died one of them would have tried to get in touch again?'

'Obviously he was too stubborn and she was too proud.'

'What makes you say she was too proud?' Meredith queried.

'A hunch that the marriage didn't work,' he replied.

'You don't know that,' Meredith pointed out. 'Maybe she was really happy with her husband.'

'And maybe he was feckless and unfaithful and walked out on her two years later,' Rhys returned mockingly.

'You're a cynic!' she accused with a laugh.

'No, I've just knocked around a bit more than you have,' he said.

She studied his carved features, his high cheekbones and the imposing line of his jaw which gave his face character. She didn't doubt he'd had plenty of experience across the whole spectrum of life, and he looked as though he'd thrived on it.

She lifted her shoulders in an attractive little shrug.

'I prefer to think the story ended my way,' she said. Ensnaring him quite unintentionally with her amber eyes, she asked, 'Or don't you believe in happy endings?'

'You do, I take it?' he said, the grooves in his lean cheeks deepening as he smiled.

'Of course,' she answered. 'I was brought up on *Snow White*, *Cinderella* and all the other fairy-stories.'

'Including the Sleeping Beauty who was woken by a kiss?' he asked.

The inflexion of his voice sent a little shiver rippling over her skin. She tilted her head to one side. 'Are you flirting with me, Rhys?' she asked, her slight huskiness genuine and very attractive.

'No more than you are with me,' he drawled.

His dark eyes held hers as he spoke, and she felt her pulse quicken strangely in response. At that moment, Jet, who had been lying beside the sofa, suddenly pricked up his ears. He raced out of the room barking noisily, and as the static in the air dispersed she said, 'That must be Dad.'

'Pity,' Rhys commented.

'I'm sorry?' she enquired.

'I was enjoying our conversation.'

She realised that she had been, too. On the spur of the moment she said, 'Are you doing anything tomorrow night, Rhys?'

'What makes you ask?' he drawled.

Her heart began to thump a little. A sense of caution told her that she would be wiser to keep

Rhys at arm's length. Recklessly she refused to heed it.

'I...I've been invited to a housewarming party. As you're new to Bryn Uchel, would you like to come with me and meet a few people?' she asked as her father strode into the room.

'Hello, Rhys. I'm sorry I wasn't here when you called,' he began briskly, his manner amiable. It was clear to Meredith from his tone that Rhys had his respect, something which was not lightly given. Gerallt glanced in her direction as he added, 'I hope my daughter's been keeping you entertained.'

A glimmer of a smile showed on Rhys's tanned face.

'She has indeed,' he agreed, his dark eyes glinting as they swivelled to her.

The devilment she saw in them convinced her he was going to decline her invitation. She should have known that, arrestingly male and interesting to talk to, he'd hardly be at a loss for company on a Saturday evening. She could have kicked herself for asking him. All she'd done was to pander to his arrogance.

Keeping her chagrin well hidden, she stood up, and said with as much poise as she could muster, 'I'll leave the two of you to talk business.'

'What time shall I pick you up Saturday evening?' Rhys asked.

Caught completely unprepared for the question, her gaze flew to his.

'Is eight o'clock OK?' he prompted, a dark eyebrow mocking her surprise.

Rallying swiftly, she said, 'Eight will be fine.'

CHAPTER FOUR

MEREDITH slipped into the gauzy midnight-blue dress she had decided to wear for the party. Its cool fabric caressed her skin, making it a perfect choice for a breathless evening.

In the distance came the uneasy rumble of summer thunder, too far off for it to herald a storm. She felt strangely jittery, as she had done all day. Stop being so silly, she told herself. She'd acted impulsively in asking Rhys to be her escort this evening, but she wasn't doing anything wrong in getting ready for their date.

She hadn't wanted to go to the party alone and, if Trefor objected, she would point out that he shouldn't have let her down at the eleventh hour. So why did she feel she was playing with danger in seeing Rhys?

She thought of the way her pulse seemed to flutter whenever her gaze collided with his. Was she really wise to be seeing him this evening? She realised that there was something about him which brought her sense of caution to the fore. He was different from any man she had ever known and she felt just a little out of her depth where he was concerned.

The sound of a car drawing up outside made her glance at the clock radio by her bed. Her inner debate meant that she hadn't allowed herself much time to get ready and now she was having to fly.

She went over to the window to look out. As she had expected, it was Rhys's car she saw pulling up on the gravel drive. She watched as he got out, arrestingly male in a linen jacket and matching beige trousers. His black hair gleamed in the sunshine as he strolled towards the porch. It crossed her mind that a panther had the same elasticity of tread, the same disturbing grace of movement.

He rang the bell and then, as he waited, he took a step back and glanced up at the house. Meredith wasn't sure whether he was admiring its mellow lines, or whether, sharply perceptive, he'd caught a glimpse of her at the window. Swiftly she drew back from her vantage point, wondering whatever she was doing spying on the man.

She crossed over to her dressing-table where, with quick, deft fingers, she twisted her silken hair into a chic knot. Her gilt tassel-drop earrings danced prettily against her cheeks as she swept her long auburn-tipped lashes with mascara. A trace of sultry shading enhanced her amber eyes, while her lips she barely augmented with a cerise lipstick.

The fragrance she was currently wearing was Ysatis. She sprayed her pulse-points lightly and then tried to unfasten the bracelet Trefor had given her. The clasp was stiff and she found she couldn't undo it.

Something sharp pricked her thumb.

'Oh, no!' she exclaimed.

The clasp, brittle with age, had snapped in her fingers, leaving the fastener embedded where it was. Now she couldn't get the bracelet off.

Not for the first time she wished Trefor hadn't bought it for her. It wasn't her style and it meant she would now have to leave her charm bracelet, which she would have preferred to have worn, in its box.

With a sigh of frustration, she collected her clutch-bag from the bed. The mirror, which caught her reflection as she left the room, showed a slim, attractive redhead. She might not have spent long changing but the effect was just the same as if she had.

Her top-knot drew attention to the lovely planes of her face, while her dress was simple but eye-catching. The fabric was so fine that it gave a suggestion of transparency, which made the skirt fall in a very flattering way. A bold yet subtle gold motif decorated the bodice and cap-like sleeves, while a hint of gold showed at her hem.

She came downstairs and went into the drawing-room. She had expected Rhys to be waiting for her and, having hurried downstairs on his account, she was disappointed to see that the drawing-room was empty save for her sister-in-law.

'Where's Rhys?' she began.

Jessica glanced up from the pages of her thriller.

'He's discussing business with Gerallt,' she answered, adding, as she took note of Meredith's appearance, 'I thought you were giving the party a miss, or has Trefor decided he can make it after all?'

'I don't know what Trefor's doing.'

'A party alone isn't much fun,' her sister-in-law commented languidly.

'Actually Rhys is taking me,' Meredith answered. She glanced at her watch. 'I hope Dad isn't going to keep him talking too long.'

'When was this arranged?' Jessica's voice was unusually sharp. 'You turned him down only the other evening.'

Puzzled by her tone, Meredith said, 'We arranged it yesterday. Why?'

'You kept that dark!' her sister-in-law said tartly.

'Not intentionally.'

'Is this a ploy to spur Trefor on with some competition or are you interested in Rhys?'

'No!' Meredith protested indignantly.

Cornflower-blue eyes that held a hard light considered her. 'No, it's not a ploy or no, you're not interested in him?' Jessica demanded.

'I find him good company.'

Her sister-in-law shut her book with a snap. 'I guessed as much,' she said. 'Well, I can't say I'm surprised. He's the first real man who's crossed your path.'

'That's not true——' Meredith began.

'Oh, you've been out with a number of boys, I grant you,' Jessica said, 'but Rhys is different. He's tough, dynamic and he goes after what he wants. But just the same I wouldn't start getting any stupid ideas about him if I were you.'

No doubt her sister-in-law meant well, but she was beginning to resent her interference.

'I'm not getting any stupid ideas——' she began and then broke off as Rhys came in.

There was nothing in the rugged planes of his face to suggest he had overheard them talking about him, but, even so, as she met his dark eyes she felt herself blush.

He let his gaze travel over her, taking in her appearance from top to toe. His look, which was sensual and flattering, seemed to knock the breath out of her for an instant.

'Am I interrupting a tête-à-tête?' Rhys teased.

Meredith's denial was contradicted by Jessica who said, with a ripple of laughter, 'You must have a sixth sense, Rhys.'

Since it was a topic best not pursued, Meredith rose quickly to her feet. 'I'm sorry I wasn't quite ready when you called,' she told him.

'You look stunning,' he replied.

'Thank you,' she said, a becoming shyness in her eyes.

'I'll let you into a secret, Rhys,' Jessica said, a thread of false humour in her voice. 'The only man Meredith's ever been ready on time for is Trefor, her steady boyfriend.'

'So it's serious between you and Trefor.' Rhys appeared amused by the information. An ironic dark eyebrow arched at Meredith. 'You'll have to tell him it's a woman's prerogative to be late.'

'I'm sure Trefor knows that,' she answered. She saw no reason to let Rhys see she was having doubts about her relationship with her boyfriend. 'He isn't a stickler for punctuality.'

'Or for keeping appointments,' Rhys observed.

'What's given you that impression?'

'Where is he tonight?'

Rather than admit she didn't know, she answered, 'Anyone can be forced to break a date.'

Rhys didn't contradict her. Instead he suggested, 'Shall we go?'

'Have a good time, the two of you,' Jessica put in sweetly.

'We'll do our best,' Meredith promised. 'See you later.'

They were in his car when Rhys said, 'What excuse did your boyfriend come up with last Saturday?'

'What do you mean, what excuse?' she asked.

'He didn't show up at the dinner party.'

Caught off guard, she said, 'How do you——?'

'So I was right in thinking Trefor was invited,' Rhys said.

She realised he had tripped her into the admission. Rather coolly she explained, 'He was held up driving back from Oxford.'

'Who by? Bandits?' Rhys mocked.

'No, roadworks!' She felt her temper rise as his dark eyes glittered infuriatingly. He was constantly making fun of her. 'You know, I'm beginning to wonder why I asked you to this party!'

'Think about it and I'm sure you'll come up with a reason,' Rhys returned calmly.

She cast a quick glance at his chiselled profile. 'What's that supposed to mean?' she asked, and found that her heart was beating skittishly.

It was as if she was afraid to examine her motives too closely. Rhys's gaze flickered towards her, a knowing glint in the depths of his cobalt eyes.

'Whose party are we going to?' he asked.

'Derec Hughes's. You met his parents last weekend,' she said. 'And you haven't answered my question.'

'I didn't think I needed to,' Rhys replied. 'You commented on the sparks between us the other evening.'

She had decided there was too much hardness in his face for him to be considered handsome, yet when he smiled he was undeniably good-looking.

'You think I'm attracted to you?' Her inflexion turned her words into a question.

Rhys slanted another glance at her.

'You behave as if you are,' he said, 'but then there's your boyfriend in the picture. I suppose he gave you the bracelet you're wearing?'

She nodded and turned her wrist. The evening sunlight glinted on the heavily tooled brass. Wondering how she was going to get it off, now that the catch had broken, she said, 'It caught his eye at an antiques fair.'

'A daintier bracelet would suit you better,' was Rhys's comment. As the powerful Jaguar slowed to pass between the tall wrought-iron gates which marked the entrance of the long drive, he asked, 'Where does your friend Derec live?'

'Not far from Bryn Uchel,' she told him. 'We go straight through the town,' she added, 'and then I'll give you directions.'

'Is it Derec's birthday?' Rhys asked.

'No, it's a housewarming party,' she explained. 'He's just moved.'

They turned on to the main road and as they did so Rhys said, 'I have to admit I'm surprised your boyfriend's so blasé about your relationship that he doesn't show up to take you to an old flame's party.'

'What makes you think Derec's an old flame?' she asked.

'Friends of the opposite sex usually are.'

'There are platonic friendships,' she insisted. 'Or don't you believe in such things?'

'I wouldn't know,' he answered, the masculine line of his mouth quirking. 'I've never had one with a woman.'

She knew from his tone he was teasing her, yet even so his remark made her pulse quicken. 'There's a first time for everything,' she said.

'Is that a challenge?' he asked, slanting an amused masculine glance at her.

'You can take it that way if you want to,' she replied and then realised that without meaning to she was flirting with him.

Rhys chuckled, and, preferring a safer topic to the one they were on, she asked, 'How are you settling in at Glan-wern? I don't think I mentioned it yesterday, but did you know Tudor Morgan used to live there?'

'No, I didn't.' He sounded interested. 'The house went out of the family, I suppose, on his death?'

She nodded. 'It's been empty most of the time since then. There was some talk of its being bought by a Swiss businessman and being turned into a hotel, but it didn't come to anything.'

'That was because I put in a higher offer,' Rhys told her.

It was news to her.

'You must have wanted Glan-wern very badly,' she said, adding with a touch of mischief, 'Or did you think that if you don't strike lucky with the exploration programme you can fall back on running a hotel?'

Rhys chuckled. 'I always strike lucky,' he drawled.

As he spoke his gaze flickered to her lips.

'Do you mean all your remarks to hold an innuendo?' she asked, playing the sophisticate.

'Interesting that you should choose to interpret them that way,' he answered lazily as he steered the Jaguar round a sharp bend.

His broad hands were tanned and capable on the wheel. She was able to imagine them being very skilled when it came to giving pleasure to a woman. Shocked at the wayward direction of her thoughts, she gave a guilty start. Her skin felt hot, and, anxious to forget that fleetingly she'd imagined Rhys touching her, she turned her head to admire the mountain scenery.

The sparks of awareness between the two of them were such that she forgot she was meant to be giving him directions.

'You should have turned left!' she said as the car overshot the junction in the road.

'We're going to my place,' Rhys told her.

'What?' she said in a startled voice, her sophisticated act of a moment ago vanishing quickly.

'I had to call in unexpectedly at the mine to check on some maintenance work and in doing so I got a smudge of oil on my shirt. I want to change it,' he said. He shot her an amused masculine glance. 'Did you think I was abducting you?'

He was making fun of her again, but the banter between them had made her warm towards him and, forgetting to take offence, she teased him back. 'You know, you'd be quite likeable if it weren't for your conceit.'

'Try to overlook it and I'll overlook your vanity,' came the mocking answer.

'What makes you think I'm vain?' she protested.

'Because you think you have a choice between me and Trefor.'

'Don't I?' she teased.

'I don't know how serious Trefor is about you,' he answered.

More importantly, she was no longer sure how serious she was about Trefor, but, enjoying Rhys's company, it was a concern she was content to shelve for the present. They came to the toll bridge and Meredith turned her head to admire the view as they crossed over it.

The river coursed gently beneath them while salt marshes stretched away on either side of its banks. Not far below the bridge, it broadened out swiftly. In the evening sunlight it was mirror-smooth, holding clear reflections of the mountains.

Rhys's house, which overlooked the estuary, was on the opposite bank from Pencarreg Hall. Hidden in elevated wooded grounds and set well back from the road, it faced west. The fiery glow of the setting sun was reflected in its elegant windows, brilliant orange against the white stone.

'I see you're having some building work done,' she said, commenting on the scaffolding at the side of the house.

'My surveyor found a number of structural faults in the house,' he answered as they went inside. 'I'm having them put right at quite some cost.'

The hall was large, with Persian rugs strewn on a black and white tiled floor. Pale walls set off classical furniture and a beautiful oak staircase. She liked the brass stair-rods and the plain red stair-carpet that complemented the dark highly polished wood.

It occurred to her suddenly that she and Rhys were completely alone together, and, in an attempt to hide an uncharacteristic flutter of nervousness, she said, 'Do you know, this is the first time I've been in Glan-wern?'

'Would you like a grand tour?' he asked. 'We've got time.'

'Yes, I should,' she said, determined to ignore her acute awareness of him physically.

He showed her into the lounge first, a very masculine room with lots of interesting abstract art on the walls. Fifteen-foot-long windows gave on to a veranda which enjoyed a breathtaking view of the estuary and mountains.

She wandered outside and stood drinking in the peace of the evening. Rhys leaned against the door-frame, watching her. She didn't need to glance at him to be conscious of his gaze on her. She found his interest in her flattering and disturbing at the same time.

A larch grew close by and she breathed in deeply, savouring its piny fragrance. Beneath its branches gnats were dancing. They looked like tiny flecks of gold in the slanting sunlight. Turning back to him, she commented, 'With some cane furniture, the veranda could be really lovely.'

'What do you mean, "could be"?' he returned as if quick to take offence.

Her amber eyes kindled with amusement.

'I wasn't criticising,' she said. 'I just meant the conservatory needs a woman's touch.'

'Move in with me and the place is all yours,' he said.

His suggestive quip made her blush prettily.

He showed her the dining-room, the study, and the large kitchen, and then announced, 'Now for the bedrooms.'

'I thought there'd be more downstairs,' she said, taken by surprise.

'That's because I haven't shown you the other wing. Remember the scaffolding?' he said as he led the way upstairs. 'As well as the structural alterations I'm having that part of the house re-wired, so it's all upside-down at the moment.'

The polished oak staircase gave on to a large square landing with bedrooms leading off. He showed them to her one after the other and then said, 'And this is the master bedroom.'

He stood back so that she could walk in. She realised that since she'd entered each of the guest rooms with him in turn to hesitate on the threshold of the master bedroom simply because it was his would make her look very prim.

'I like your taste,' she said, striving to forget her awareness of his male presence.

In such an intimate setting, it wasn't easy. His bedroom, which was spacious, was decorated in blues. There was a beautiful Persian carpet on the floor and heavily draped curtains framed the windows. The mahogany furniture added to the very masculine feel of the room.

A geometrically patterned blue duvet covered the large double bed. Meredith's gaze skittered towards it. Even with so much space, the bed seemed to dominate the room. Slightly unsure of herself and, not wanting Rhys to know it, she went over to the window, feigning an interest in the view which she had already admired from the lounge.

The sun had dipped now behind the mountains and the stormy sky was streaked with reds and gold. The thick carpeting made his footfall soundless, yet in every nerve she sensed his approach. He came and stood beside her, the spicy aroma of his aftershave adding to her awareness of him.

'I could gaze at this view for ever,' she murmured, a pulse pitter-pattering strangely at the base of her neck.

'Feel free,' he answered.

He moved away and, finding it easier to breathe again, she said, 'It's lovely here looking out over the estuary but don't you find the place very big for one?'

'I'd rather have too much space than too little,' he replied, 'but you're right, it's a family house.'

'There are plenty of other places on the market. What made you decide...?' she began as she turned back to him, the words locking in her throat as she saw that he had discarded his jacket and was in the process of changing his shirt.

Half stripped, strength and power showed in every line of him. The bronzed muscles of his shoulders were full and round while those of his chest, with its tangle of dark hair, were broad and flat.

Realising she was staring, she quickly raised her gaze to his. 'I...I was saying...' she faltered.

'You do things to me when you look at me like that,' Rhys murmured huskily.

She took a step in retreat as he came towards her, and then gave a little gasp as the wall grazed her back.

'I don't mean to,' she said in a whisper, trapped in more ways than one. 'Rhys...'

'Don't you, my amber-eyed witch?' he muttered, pulling her into his arms and tilting up her chin.

She felt the hardness of his thighs brush hers and her heartbeat quickened dizzily. Everything in the room seemed to fade from her vision except for Rhys's chiselled face. She drank in the strong lines of his cheekbones and jaw, the dimple in his chin, his sensual lips.

'I . . . I'm not your amber-eyed witch,' she said raggedly, suddenly in the grip of an enchantment that made her scarcely aware of where she was or what she was saying.

'Not yet, perhaps,' he said, his eyes as dark as ink.

A shaft of weakness pierced her as his gaze slid to her mouth. She knew he was going to kiss her, knew it and, held fast by some kind of spell, wanted him to. The pressure of his hand on her waist increased to draw her into his embrace.

He bent his head, his mouth touching hers, briefly, gently, before parting her lips with a swift intensity that sent a tide of pleasure, hot and exciting, racing along her veins. There was a roaring in her ears like the pounding of the sea. She felt as if she were drowning, the possessiveness of his kiss blinding her to everything save the language of desire.

She could think of nothing save the nearness of his body, the caress of his hand at the base of her spine and her desire for him to go on kissing her with such demanding intensity. As his mouth explored hers, long and insatiably, she melted into his arms, the slightness of her body fitting perfectly against his lean taut frame.

She had never dreamed that desire could be so fierce and elemental. She was trembling from its force when he finally raised his head.

During their kiss reality had been swept away by the magic of the moment. Now, as her lashes fluttered up, time and place began to return. Feeling as if she had just come off a roller-coaster, she lifted her bewildered gaze to meet the cobalt glitter in Rhys's eyes. His expression was enigmatic as he studied her flushed face and took note of her breathing, which was as altered as his own.

'Enough, or are you as hungry for more as I am?' he asked huskily.

Her hands, which had been up around his neck, came down to wedge a space between them. Devastated by the primitive need which had compelled her to yield to his kiss when less than a week before she had believed she was in love with Trefor, she said shakenly, 'Let . . . let go of me.'

The line of his sensual mouth quirked mockingly, but he made no attempt to thwart her as she pushed against the bronzed muscles of his chest. Freed from his embrace, she warned, frightened by the feelings he had unlocked within her, 'You mustn't ever kiss me like that again.'

'If it's serious between you and Trefor you'd better not let me,' he returned, one dark brow lifting slightly.

She blushed hotly. She had never lost control to any man as she had to him just now and she couldn't think of one word to say in reply. Rhys watched her.

'For once it seems you're stuck for an answer,' he mocked.

All along she'd been certain he was used to women throwing themselves into his arms. She'd

also thought that she was different! Aghast that
she had kissed him back so sweetly and with such
need, she tried to feign nonchalance.

'I'll wait for you downstairs,' she said. 'If we
don't hurry we'll be late for the party.'

She felt his masculine gaze between her
shoulder-blades as she went to the door, and
hoped he didn't know that her calm exit from his
bedroom was in reality a confused flight. She
went downstairs and into the lounge, where she
leaned against the wall and closed her eyes. If
she was to stop shaking, she desperately needed
a moment or two to herself to recover from
Rhys's assault on her senses.

CHAPTER FIVE

THE music from the stereo was loud. With the party in full swing the beat competed with the clamour of talk and laughter. Some of the chattering guests stood round the bar in the lounge, others were serving themselves from the buffet table in the dining-room. The french windows were open on to the garden and several couples were dancing on the patio.

'Since you brought me here ostensibly to introduce me to everyone, where do we start?' Rhys drawled.

Meredith wasn't sure what he meant by his cryptic use of the word 'ostensibly'.

'I told you why...' she began.

Before she could finish, one of the guests, a pretty brunette, intruded on their conversation.

'Shame on you, Meredith, monopolising the most handsome man at the party,' she chided. Her lips curved as she turned to Rhys. 'Hi, I'm Tracy Thomas. I don't think we've met before.'

'We haven't or I'd have remembered,' Rhys said. He was very urbane, Meredith thought, struck as ever by his easy manner as he introduced himself to the other woman. 'How do you do? I'm Rhys Treherne.'

'The mining engineer!' Tracy warbled, as she placed him.

'The same,' he said.

'I imagine you and Meredith must have quite a bit in common as you're on the board with her father,' the brunette commented, a trace of speculation in her dark brown eyes as she glanced between the two of them.

'You could say that,' Rhys agreed.

His inflexion made Meredith's skin prickle. She took a sip of her drink.

'Derec really knows how to give a party,' she murmured, wanting Rhys to think she had taken his kiss far too lightly to be disturbed by any subtly mocking reference to it.

'Doesn't he?' Tracy agreed. She glanced round the crowded lounge as she asked, 'Where's Trefor tonight?'

Since Tracy was inquisitive, Meredith was prepared for the question.

'He——' she began.

'He's elsewhere, fortunately for me,' Rhys cut in.

He drew Meredith to his side as he spoke. She started slightly and would have shied away, but the firm hand on her waist was implacable.

'I hadn't realised you'd broken up with Trefor,' Tracy said, jumping swiftly to conclusions.

'I . . . I haven't,' she said, sounding rather flustered, because Rhys had only to touch her to make her pulse jump nervously.

'Yet.' His comment implied that it was only a matter of time.

'I see,' Tracy said meaningfully, drifting away.

The moment the brunette had left them, Meredith protested, pushing at his arm, 'You had

no right to say what you did in front of Tracy.
Now she thinks...'

'Does it matter what she thinks?' Rhys asked.

'Yes... No...' she contradicted herself.

Not certain what she meant, she broke off.
Even without Tracy to spread the word, news that
she'd turned up at the housewarming in the
company of a tall magnetic stranger was bound
to get back to Trefor, she realised. And what was
she going to tell him when it did? She wasn't sure
since she hadn't bargained for ending up in
Rhys's embrace, as she had a short while ago at
his house.

Try as she might, she couldn't come up with
one single explanation as to why she had allowed
him to kiss her. A blush warmed her cheeks as
she remembered how willing she had been. He
hadn't snatched her into his arms. He hadn't used
any force at all. If he had she wouldn't be feeling
so confused now.

You're making too much of it, an inner voice
insisted. For a few dizzy moments she'd been
carried away, that was all. Rhys's virile magnetism was strong and she wasn't quite as immune
to it as she'd thought.

'Have you made up your mind yet?' Rhys said,
his dark eyes mocking her.

Afraid that telepathy had enabled him to read
her thoughts, she misunderstood him. 'About
you and me?' she asked, and then could have
bitten her tongue.

She didn't realise that her question, far from
giving her away, had a flirtatious charm.

'I won't ask you what your decision is,' he murmured with an amused chuckle as another couple came up to join them.

Other guests quickly gravitated in their direction. Rhys was good company and the conversation was lively with plenty of laughter. The party mood was infectious and gradually Meredith began to relax and enjoy herself.

It was crazy to let one kiss make her feel so shaken and confused. She told herself firmly to forget it.

'Another drink?' Rhys asked a short while later as she drained her glass.

'Yes, but it's OK, I'll get it,' she told him.

She'd only just left his side when she was waylaid by Derec Hughes. Very like his father, Evan, in both looks and manner, he had dark hair, a strong jaw and a wide humorous mouth. He and Meredith had been in the same class at school and then at university together. Theirs had always been an uncomplicated relationship; they were just friends who shared a similar background.

'I like your choice of house,' she said.

'Yes, it's not bad, but I'm planning a few alterations here and there, the first one being to decorate the dining-room. All those giant peonies on the wallpaper!'

'It is a bit overpowering,' Meredith agreed with a laugh, and then wondered how it was she could talk with Derec without the atmosphere becoming dangerously charged whereas with Rhys, even without flirting, the atmosphere seemed to vibrate between them.

As she and Derec crossed the lounge together he asked, 'What's happened to Trefor? Have you sent him packing?'

'You're the second person to ask me that,' she said.

'Well, if you have you don't seem to be pining for him,' Derec observed. 'A brand new dress, I see, and a brand new escort. The dress certainly suits you. Not having spoken to him yet, I don't know about the escort. Who is he?'

She wasn't sure about her escort either, in more ways than one. In particular she wasn't sure about her feelings for him. It was something she preferred not to dwell on.

'He's the new engineer at the mine.'

'Of course, I should have guessed,' he said. 'He looks like someone who's used to being in charge. Now, what are you drinking?'

They chatted while he poured her a drink.

'I see we're almost out of ice,' he said. 'Don't go away and I'll fetch some more from the fridge.'

He was gone a little time and while she was waiting Meredith glanced through Derec's collection of LPs.

'Are you hunting up a slow number for us to dance to?' Rhys's voice sounded at her elbow.

'I'm waiting for Derec to come back with my drink,' she told him, her pulse affected by the strain of remaining indifferent to his masculine presence.

'I thought maybe you were hiding from me,' he replied.

They were standing very close to the stereo and she missed what he said next. He put his hand on her back to steer her somewhere quieter, his palm warm against her spine.

'You seem a little off balance this evening,' he observed.

If she was, the fault was his.

'Why would I be off balance?' she challenged him to explain. 'And why are you marching me off into the kitchen? I thought you came here with me so I could introduce you to people.'

'I've already been introduced to the person I'm interested in,' he answered.

'You mean Tracy,' Meredith hazarded a guess and was annoyed with herself for feeling faintly slighted that, when she had brought him to the party, he had his eyes on another girl.

In the kitchen Rhys leaned against the worktop. The sounds of the party were muted, somehow emphasising the fact that they were alone together.

'You're not blonde, so don't act dumb,' he said lazily. 'The person I'm interested in is you.'

She felt her heartbeat quicken. She was flattered and yet at the same time she was aware of a strange inclination to escape back to the lounge. She could easily do so under the pretext of finding Derec, who must be looking for her with her drink, but since she'd never taken flight from any man before she stood her ground and said, 'I can't help but think you've said that to a lot of women.'

Rhys's wolfish grin was attractive. 'Quite a few,' he admitted.

'I'll bet!' She found she hated them all and him, too, for an instant for thinking he could use the same line on her.

'Let's talk about you and Trefor, rather than you and me,' he said. 'How long have you been going out with him?'

Her relationship with her boyfriend had suited her well until Rhys had appeared on the scene. Faintly annoyed with him for unsettling her, she said, 'Two years. Not that it's any affair of yours.'

'Don't get defensive,' Rhys ordered. 'I'm trying to understand you.'

'I prefer to be a woman of mystery,' she said and headed for the door.

'Or are you frightened what you might discover about yourself if we go on talking?' he drawled.

He had hit a nerve, and her reaction to his question showed it. 'What are you hinting at?' she demanded.

'I'm not hinting at anything,' Rhys said. 'Jessica tells me you're serious about Trefor, but are you?'

'I...' She had been until Rhys had come into her life, very serious.

'When a romance drags on for two years without getting anywhere, it's sometimes because one of the partners would like to get out of it but doesn't have the courage to do so.'

The conclusion she jumped to was that he was referring to her boyfriend and, as much to save face as anything else, she said, 'Trefor loves me.'

'He has a funny way of showing it, then. He's never around,' Rhys reminded her. At that moment the doorbell buzzed. 'Unless that's him, of course, come just in time to take you home.'

She did not appreciate his mockery.

'It isn't Trefor's fault that some weekends he has to work,' she said, stating what was a surmise as if it were a fact.

It was humiliating the way her boyfriend was making it look to everyone, Rhys included, as if he was taking her for granted at best and losing interest in her at worst.

'You'll have to find some feminine wile to bring him back to heel,' Rhys said sardonically to her as the bell rang a second time.

His mockery invariably set the match to her temper.

'Trefor isn't roaming. He's working,' she said tartly. 'And now, if you'll excuse me, as no one else seems to have heard the bell, I'll go and answer the door.'

With that she swept into the hall. It was in her mind that when she next saw Trefor she was going to tell him she'd put up with as much as she was going to of his cavalier treatment.

She opened the front door to welcome the late-comer to the throng and then felt her heart give a tiny lurch of dismayed surprise. Her boyfriend stood outside. He was dressed casually in a Pringle shirt and pullover and dark blue trousers and was carrying a bottle of red wine, his contribution to the housewarming.

'T. . . Trefor!' she began, guilt overtaking her anger.

Obviously he'd rushed straight over from the hospital and now she felt awful that, although she'd defended him to Rhys, she'd maligned him in her own thoughts.

'Hi,' he smiled as he bent to kiss her. 'Surprised?'

'Yes,' she admitted with an awkward little laugh. She offered him her cheek. Trefor didn't insist on a more intimate embrace, but now she felt doubly guilty. Why had she evaded his lips? Did she think he would know from her kiss she had been in Rhys's arms?

'How . . . how did you manage to get here after all?' she faltered.

'Didn't I promise I wouldn't let you down?' he said with a smile.

'Yes, but then you left a message saying you couldn't make it,' she reminded him in her own defence.

'There's a long story behind that message,' he said with rueful humour. 'I'll explain later.'

She drew a deep breath. The only thing to do was to get it over with and confess that on the spur of the moment she'd asked Rhys to be her escort.

'I've got something to explain too,' she admitted. 'I . . . I thought you'd broken your promise——'

'It was close,' he laughed, cutting in. 'That's why I'm late. I guessed you'd come to the party on your own so——'

'As it happens, in fact, she came with me.' A male voice that was faintly sardonic corrected his assumption.

Meredith pivoted sharply to see Rhys, his tall virile figure framed by the kitchen door. He measured up her boyfriend with his gaze, the glint in his cobalt eyes suggesting that he found the sum total of little account.

Trefor's mouth tightened. 'And who exactly——?' he began, clipping out the words.

Meredith intervened quickly. She didn't want the two men sparring off against each other. Instinct told her who would be the victor, if it came to a fight of any sort and it wouldn't be her boyfriend.

'I . . . I don't think you've had a chance to meet Rhys yet, have you, Trefor?' she put in hurriedly. 'I asked him to bring me this evening because I thought you couldn't make it.'

'Whatever kept you must have been important,' Rhys drawled.

Trefor clearly didn't appreciate the gibe but evidently he concurred with Meredith's estimation of Rhys and, having been put in the picture, he kept his hostility polite.

'It was,' he agreed, 'but better late than never.'

A slender blonde appeared at that moment from the lounge.

'Better never late,' she made the giggling comment as she butted in. 'Meredith, Derec's looking for you. You owe him a dance, or something.'

'No, it's me she owes the dance,' Rhys said. 'Do you have any objections, Trefor?'

His tone made it clear his question was one of form and, with little option to do otherwise, Trefor gave the conventional answer.

'Go ahead.'

Rhys held out his hand. Meredith went towards him, accepting his guiding hand on her back. Since she'd asked him to be her partner at the party, she couldn't very well refuse to dance with him even had she wished to. Yet he unsettled her and a slow number would remind her inevitably of those few heady minutes when she had been in his arms.

Rhys guided her through the lounge and outside on to the patio. With its romantic shadows it made an excellent dance-floor. The sky was dark now, like midnight-blue velvet, and the coloured lights, which were strung from the house and down the garden, shone like stars that twinkled overhead.

'"Lying Eyes",' Rhys commented on the music that was playing as he gathered her towards him. 'The very track I'd have chosen myself.'

She was completely at a loss to understand why the record prompted Rhys to give her such a searching look, and she blushed, partly because she failed to grasp what he was driving at, but mainly because of the effect his closeness had on her senses.

'Do you like the Eagles?' she asked, trying to clarify things.

Her question earned her a cynically amused quirk of one dark eyebrow.

'You know, you're very good,' Rhys applauded.

'What do you mean?' she asked.

'I would have thought it was obvious,' Rhys returned. 'Are you going to come clean with

Trefor and tell him about our interlude at sunset?' he asked.

His reminder of their kiss threw her into confusion.

'P . . . possibly,' she stammered.

'And if that doesn't work?' Rhys asked.

It was a gibe, she was sure, and she was tempted to ignore his question, but curiosity got the better of her.

'If what doesn't work?' she asked.

'Your little act where you throw yourself at me to make Trefor jealous.'

Her startled gaze went to his. As she missed a step Rhys's arms tightened around her. It wasn't at all the way he made it sound but she coloured as hotly as if she were guilty as charged. Making Trefor jealous had never crossed her mind, and she hadn't thrown herself at Rhys!

'I don't know where you've got your facts from——' she began.

'Have you forgotten your tête-à-tête with Jessica? Your sister-in-law's voice carries very clearly,' he mocked.

She remembered her sister-in-law's accusation, which she had denied. 'Eavesdroppers——' she began angrily.

'Sometimes hear things that are most enlightening,' he drawled, cutting in.

'And sometimes they get their facts wrong!'

'Do you mean to say you didn't know Trefor was going to roll up this evening?' Rhys asked sardonically. 'It's fairly obvious your boyfriend's been taking you for granted, and playing one man off against another is the oldest feminine trick in the book.'

'It may be, but it isn't one of my tricks,' Meredith said hotly. 'I asked you if you'd come with me solely because I don't like going to parties alone.'

'I suppose you kissed me with that in mind, too,' Rhys taunted.

The taunt was too much for her. Angry, she snatched herself out of his arms, only to give a gasp as her wrist was imprisoned and she was spun back towards him.

'I'm not dancing with you any more!' she flared.

'It's more than time someone took you in hand.' Rhys's tone was amused, but there was a hard light in his eyes.

Intuition warned her that he'd force her to make a scene before he'd release her. It added to her fury that, when he hadn't even raised his voice, she somehow didn't dare defy him.

'Well, it won't be you,' she said in a mutinous undertone. 'I can promise you that!'

'And I can promise you it won't be Trefor. If he was a man he wouldn't need to be spurred on with competition.'

'I've already told you,' she flashed. 'I'm not trying to make Trefor jealous.'

'Not when you knew he'd roll up late?' Rhys was scathing. 'You know, I'm surprised that a woman like you needs to resort to playing games.'

His answer made it obvious that, despite what she'd said, he was determined to think the worst of her. Oddly enough, it really hurt.

'Think what you like,' she sparked. 'I'm not accountable to you!'

'No, you're not,' he agreed. As he spoke his hand on her back drew her closer to avoid her colliding with another couple. 'But, just the same, before you go on chasing after Trefor I'd do a bit of heartsearching if I were you.'

'I don't need your advice,' she flashed back, 'And I'm not chasing Trefor.'

'It will be interesting to see whether or not you manage to land him,' Rhys mocked.

The sparks were beginning to fly between them in earnest, and it was only because she guessed if she flared with another answer he'd cap it with another gibe that she mastered the impulse to continue sparring with him. To add to the fury inside her, Rhys's manner was far too intimate.

'You're holding me too close!' she hissed under her breath.

'Not for me I'm not,' he taunted, 'And not for you either, if you're honest. Your trembling gives you away.'

It was all she could do not to slap him.

'You really think you're God's gift, don't you?' she retorted, furious that he knew the effect he had on her senses, and furious too because she couldn't give rein to her temper in front of the other guests.

The music came to an end and Rhys released her. The glitter in his eyes in contrast to his drawl, he said, 'You run along back to Trefor. Having got him here and made him nicely jealous, you don't want to waste what's left of the evening.'

A suitable parting shot eluded her. She gave Rhys an icy stare and returned to the lounge, where Trefor was talking to Derec. Fuming over the conclusion Rhys had chosen to jump to about her, she walked past her boyfriend without noticing him.

His hand shot out, drawing her to his side. He had the look of a man trying to appear relaxed and pleasant when underneath he was fed up and annoyed. Jokingly he said to Derec, 'I'm sorry we're going to have to leave as soon as I've arrived, but I didn't mean to get here so late.'

'I'm glad you were able to look in,' Derec answered. He kissed Meredith on the cheek. 'It was nice to see you again.'

In the car she began, guessing that trouble was brewing and in no mood for it, 'I know what you're thinking——'

'We'll discuss this when we get to the pub,' Trefor interrupted.

The White Hart, which fronted on to the river, was very popular, especially in summer. On Saturday evenings it was always crowded. The buzz of voices mingled with the music, provided by a very talented local band, and the atmosphere, as ever, was carefree and convivial.

'Let's take our drinks outside,' Trefor said.

They found an empty table on the terrace and, guessing what was coming, Meredith began in defence of herself,

'I know you're angry with me, but there was no reason why I shouldn't have asked Rhys to come with me to the party. It was only to introduce him to a few people.'

'I think Rhys is quite capable of introducing himself,' Trefor said, scowling. 'From what I've seen of him, he's not only confident, he's the sort to grab what he wants.'

Meredith fingered her glass as she remembered the way he had kissed her. Ought she to make a clean breast of it and confess, or was there no need to since she had no intention of ever allowing Rhys to kiss her again?

Trefor took hold of her hand, his tone softening as he misread her mutinous expression.

'Just as long as Rhys realises you're my girl,' he said. 'And I think it's time we got engaged.'

'But...' she faltered, taken unawares.

'But what?' he wanted to know.

'We...we don't have to get engaged for everyone to know I'm your girl.' Without knowing why, Meredith found herself suddenly trying to keep things as they were between them.

'Well, let's take it a step further,' Trefor said. 'Will you marry me?'

In the midst of her surprise the irony of it all struck her. Jessica had accused her of trying to make Trefor jealous and Rhys had chosen to believe it of her, too. They were both wrong, and yet here Trefor was proposing to her!

Had he asked her a week ago she would have answered yes willingly, she was sure. Yet now she hesitated. What was wrong with her? she wondered in a panic.

Surely she wasn't letting a kiss from a man she'd first met last Saturday influence her reply. Right now at the party he was probably kissing some other girl, as undoubtedly he had kissed girls in South Africa and Canada, girls he had forgotten, but who hadn't forgotten him.

'I . . . I can't give you an answer just like that on the spot,' she stammered. 'Marriage is serious, Trefor. It's for life. We've got to be a hundred per cent sure we're right for each other.'

'So you're asking for time?' he said.

'Y. . . yes.' Time to do some heartsearching, she thought, and then realised to her chagrin that it was precisely what Rhys had suggested.

CHAPTER SIX

IN SPITE of the sunlight which flooded her bedroom, Meredith got up on Monday morning feeling that the day was bound to be tinged with sadness for her. Had he not been killed in a car accident it would have been Stephen's twenty-eighth birthday.

She guessed, though her father made no mention of the date as they chatted over breakfast, that Stephen was as much in his mind as he was in hers. They talked generally of other things; the price of gold, the pound against the dollar, the planned visit of Gerallt's sister in a few weeks' time.

She and her husband were coming over from their home in California. Until the summer before they had been rather shadowy figures in Meredith's life. She had been very young when they had visited before and, despite their letters, she'd felt she hardly knew them.

That had all altered when she had flown out to stay with them in their beautiful house which overlooked the ocean. They'd given her the most wonderful holiday. It had been a real chance for her to get to know them properly and she was delighted that they'd taken up Gerallt's invitation.

She was finishing her coffee when her sister-in-law joined them. Jessica liked a leisurely start to the morning and that was the usual pattern of things.

'You two are just off, I suppose,' she began as she took her place at the breakfast table.

'Yes, rushed as usual,' Gerallt said as he went out. Since he would have loathed it any other way it was a joking comment, not a complaint.

'What are your plans for today?' Meredith asked her sister-in-law as she pushed back her chair.

Jessica sipped her orange juice.

'I shall do some shopping,' she answered. 'I'd like some more sandals. I haven't a pair to go with the last dress I bought. And then I'm seeing Rhys for lunch. I have a proposition I want to put to him.'

'What sort of a proposition?' Meredith immediately wanted to know.

Jessica smiled a secret smile. 'That's classified at the moment.'

'At least give me a clue,' Meredith said, her curiosity awoken.

Jessica shook her head. 'You'll have to wait and see,' she said.

Meredith collected some music from the drawing-room, adding it to the base of a pile of exercise books she'd left by the phone, as her father came into the hall. They left the house together.

It was a lovely morning, and the sun seemed very bright after the dimness of the porch.

'It looks as if you're going to need a lift to school this morning,' Gerallt remarked, directing her gaze to her black Peugeot, which was parked on the gravel drive. One of the rear tyres was completely flat.

'Oh, no!' she exclaimed. 'What's caused that, do you think?'

'It could be a faulty valve,' Gerallt speculated, going over to inspect the flat tyre. He quickly spotted the rusty nail that was embedded in the tread. Drawing her attention to it, he said, 'No, it's an ordinary puncture.'

'I must have picked that nail up yesterday driving home,' she sighed.

Her father checked his watch.

'If I change the tyre for you now we'll both be late,' he said, 'and I've a board meeting at nine. In any case I'd prefer you to have a new tyre fitted. I don't like patched-up spares. I'll try to get someone to come out from the garage later on today.'

'I'd be glad if it could be done today,' Meredith said, her arms folded around the books she was carrying. 'I rely on the car so much.'

As they moved off down the drive in her father's Range Rover, he remarked,

'You've got a slight dent in the side of your bumper. Did you know?'

'The other Saturday I misjudged the amount of space I'd got to manoeuvre,' she said, and thought of Rhys.

He hadn't told her yet what the estimate was on his car.

'It's not much, but you may as well get it fixed at the same time,' Gerallt said.

'Good idea,' she agreed.

The strong masculine face which had come into her mind was hard to dislodge, and as they sped along the main road she remarked, 'I imagine Rhys Treherne is making his mark at the mine. Is it a case of new brooms sweeping clean?'

'He's a worker, that boy,' her father answered, approval in his voice. 'He may be a hard taskmaster but he demands no more from other people than he expects from himself.'

The ghost of a wry smile touched Meredith's lips at hearing Rhys described as a boy. Arrogant and very cutting at times, there was nothing the least bit boyish about him in her estimation!

'He won't be very popular if he turns out to be a slave-driver,' she commented, scoring a subtle dig against him.

His comments to her at the party still rankled.

'I'd be surprised if Rhys cares very much about popularity,' Gerallt answered. 'What's important to him is getting the job done well and done quickly. He reminds me quite a lot of myself at his age.'

'Then I'm glad you've changed,' Meredith declared, 'though I can't believe you ever had his sarcastic sense of humour!'

Her father slanted an amused glance in her direction.

'I should have thought you would have admired his drive and ambition. Besides,' he said, querying her avowal that she didn't like Rhys, 'didn't you go out with him on Saturday?'

'That's a long story,' she answered.

'What am I to make of that remark?' her father asked.

'Rhys has a very low opinion of me,' she answered. 'He overheard something Jessica said and chose to misinterpret it.'

'Well, when he gets to know you better his opinion will soon change.'

'I don't intend to let him get to know me better,' Meredith said.

'I see. It's like that, is it?' Gerallt said, amused by her vehemence.

'Yes, it is,' she answered.

'What time do you want me to pick you up this evening?' her father asked as he drew up outside the school gates.

Meredith thought for a moment. 'I'm fitting in another rehearsal for the school concert and then... Can you pick me up at six?' she said as she decided.

She didn't say so, but when the concert rehearsal was over she intended visiting the churchyard to lay some flowers on Stephen's grave.

St Mary's wasn't far from the town centre and when she finished work it didn't take her long to walk there from school. The granite church, which had been built in the twelfth century, was set well back from the road. A pretty lych gate led to the church porch, while on either side of the sunlit path weathered granite tombs stood as they had for years among the neatly trimmed grass.

Behind the church the ground rose fairly steeply, giving a dramatic view of the mountains across the valley. Heather shaded the slopes with pink and lavender, the pristine colours of the landscape matched by an equally pristine sky.

It was some distance from the lych gate to the more recent graves on the hillside. Meredith arranged the flowers she had bought in the town and set the vase on her brother's grave. Then she sat for a while on a seat in the bright sunshine.

The ache beneath her ribs seemed intensified by the solitude. She swallowed hard and blinked against the prickle of tears. Stephen had been so full of life and she missed him. It was so hard to accept that he was gone forever.

The panorama of mountains blurred as, unable to help herself, she began to weep. When she finally steadied and dried her eyes with her handkerchief she felt calmer. It was better to give way to her emotions here rather than at home. She didn't want to make today worse for either her father or her sister-in-law by breaking down in tears.

She was walking back along the path when to her surprise she noticed the tall figure of Rhys Treherne. He was standing at the side of the church reading the inscription on one of the tombstones. She didn't think he had seen her and for an irrational instant she was tempted to avoid him by slipping round by the other side of the building.

Quelling the foolish impulse, she continued resolutely along the path. Rhys glanced up, watching her indolently as she approached. She didn't show it, but she felt strangely and annoyingly jittery under the gaze of those keen cobalt eyes.

The granite headstone he'd been looking at belonged to Tudor Morgan, who had died aged seventy-five.

'Boning up on local history?' she said as she went to walk past him.

'Why not ask what I'm doing here if that's what you're wondering?'

His mockery drew her to a halt.

'All right, I'll admit I'm curious,' she said, her chin tilting as she looked up at him. 'You don't strike me as the sort of person who'd enjoy a leisurely wander round a country churchyard.'

Against her will she noted how the sunlight gleamed on his black hair. As ever, the impact of his virile magnetism was impossible to ignore. His perfectly cut jacket was open to show a classic striped shirt and diamond-patterned silk tie. Wanting to find fault with him, she decided that a plain tie would have been a better choice.

'Were you hoping that as I drove past I spotted you in that very eye-catching dress you're wearing and decided to stop for a chat?' he said.

In spite of herself her temper flared a little. 'You really are the most conceited man I've ever met!'

A dark eyebrow quirked mockingly. 'And you're very fiery, though not with the boyfriend, I notice.'

'Trefor doesn't set out to provoke me!' she said.

'Trefor doesn't set out to do much at all.' Rhys's laconic answer told her exactly what he thought of her boyfriend.

She was tempted to tell him that Trefor had in fact proposed to her, but as she knew the reaction she could expect if she did she held her tongue.

'What excuse did he give you to explain why he showed up late at the party when he'd said he couldn't make it?' Rhys asked.

Experience had taught her that sparring with him only led to sparks in the air and intuition told her that such sparks were potentially dangerous. Yet the impulse to return the gibe was too much.

'One that satisfied me,' she said, and added, 'And Trefor wasn't terribly taken with you either.'

She intended her rejoinder as a parting shot, but instead Rhys fell smoothly into step with her. His hand touching her elbow, he said, 'You must tell me what he intends to do about it while I run you home.'

'I don't need you to run me home, thank you,' she answered coolly. 'My father's giving me a lift.'

'He told me,' Rhys said. 'But he's been held up at the office, so I said I'd drive you. It was lucky I spotted you. Your father said he was meeting you outside the school.'

As he spoke he swung the lych gate open for her. Damn, she thought, now I've got to be grateful! A glimmer of an amused smile touched the masculine line of his mouth. She was sure he knew full well that she had no desire to be indebted to him, but she managed, 'It's kind of you to give me a lift, but really there was no need for you to bother. I could have caught the bus.'

'You'd find it a long walk from the bus stop, especially since it must be half a mile to your house up your drive,' he returned.

He had parked right outside the church. The sun roof was open, and a pleasant rush of air fanned her face as they pulled away.

'Do you always work so late?' Rhys asked, his gaze flickering towards her. 'I thought teachers were supposed to have easy hours.'

'Why? Are you thinking of a change of career?'

Her question drew an amused smile from him.

'No, teaching's a vocation,' he said. 'I'll stick to what I know.'

'According to my father you know your job inside out,' she remarked, brushing back a strand of hair as it blew across her face.

'Is that why you resent me, Meredith?'

His unexpected question made her glance in his direction. His face in profile was very strong, his jawline aggressive, the set of his mouth sensual yet firm.

'Why should I resent you?' she asked. It was an honest question; she wasn't bluffing.

'How about for usurping Stephen's position at the mine?' he suggested.

'My brother's dead,' she pointed out.

'I know,' Rhys said. 'Do you often visit his grave?'

His voice was oddly gentle, and, afraid that her own might waver if she explained that today was special, she said, meaning it, 'I don't resent you because of Stephen. My brother worked hard for the company. You're continuing his work by putting the exploration programme into effect.'

'I'm glad that's the way you see it,' Rhys replied. 'I don't want there to be a wedge between us.'

She glanced at him, wondering what to make of his comment. Deciding to sound him out for curiosity's sake, she said,

'Do you care whether I resent you or not?'

His cobalt gaze slanted towards her. 'Ought I to be flattered by that question?' he drawled.

'I don't follow you,' she said.

'I thought perhaps you were trying to work out whether or not I'm interested in you,' he mocked.

'Well, I wasn't!' Meredith snapped, blushing a little.

Annoyed that he seemed to think she was attracted to him, she turned her head, pretending that her attention was caught by the view of the estuary. It was low tide and the golden sand banks in mid-stream seemed almost to bask in the sun which glinted off the water.

Since there was no taking it off, she was wearing the Victorian bracelet Trefor had given her, but she didn't realise she was fingering it until Rhys asked, 'Is the slave bracelet chafing your wrist?'

'It's not a slave bracelet,' she corrected him.

'I note there's still no engagement ring to go with it,' he commented. 'I thought your little ploy on Saturday might have prompted your boyfriend to pop the question.'

'You're insufferable!' she exclaimed. 'I explained to you on Saturday that I wasn't angling for a proposal from him——'

Her words cut no ice with Rhys, who interrupted mockingly, 'What do you plan to do now to spur him on?'

'It may interest you to know,' she said, her temper getting the better of her, 'that Trefor asked me to marry him after the party.'

A sharp glance was slanted in her direction. She saw the masculine line of Rhys's mouth quirk sardonically.

'Well, well!' he commented.

It was amazing the degree of amused derision he could inject into just two words.

'I knew that would be your reaction!' she said angrily, all the more stung by it because through no fault of her own the case did look black against her. 'You think I engineered what happened, but I had no idea that Trefor would turn up as he did!'

'My word, you certainly kept it dark,' Rhys said.

'I kept it dark because I knew how hateful you'd be,' she retorted. 'And just to prove it wasn't my *ploy*, as you choose to call it, let me tell you that I haven't accepted him.'

A speculative frown appeared between Rhys's brows.

'Why did you turn him down?' he wanted to know.

'I... I felt I needed more time.'

The line of Rhys's mouth quirked.

'Perhaps you should have made sure of him while you had the chance,' he said.

Strangely it didn't sound like a gibe.

'I don't follow you,' she told him.

'Think about it,' he drawled.

She still didn't get the gibe. All she knew was that in every conversation they ever had something unnamed and unpredictable vibrated in the air. It was the reason she remained silent as the Jaguar purred up the long drive.

'Well, here we are,' Rhys drawled as the house came into sight.

'Thanks for running me home.'

Her words were polite; her tone rather distant.

'You're very attractive when you put on that cool haughty manner,' he observed. The car came to a smooth halt on the gravel. 'In fact, you're very attractive altogether.'

The line of his mouth was suspiciously firm.

'Are you making fun of me again?' she demanded, hating the way that he was able to laugh at her and yet quicken her pulse with the sensual note in his voice at the same time.

'Perish the thought,' he chuckled.

Amber sparks in her eyes, she collected her shoulder-bag from the dashboard and got out of his car. Jet came bounding out of the porch to greet her as she walked towards the house, her hair shining like copper in the sunlight. As if Rhys's mockery had failed to raise her temperature, she bent to make a fuss of the excited dog.

She expected to hear the roar of acceleration but instead of his car pulling away there was the sound of the driver's door shutting. Glancing up, she saw him striding in her direction. For an instant she thought it was on her account and then she realised that Jessica was cutting across the lawn.

She looked stunning as usual in a tailored shirt-dress that showed off her slim figure. Raising her hand to wave, she called, 'Hello, Rhys.'

'Hi,' he said. 'I was wondering if I could pick up that album you mentioned.'

'Of course,' Jessica purred. 'Rhys wants to borrow the album Stephen had which shows the mine as it was in the early 1900s,' she explained to Meredith.

'It's 1912 I'm particularly curious about,' he said.

Meredith, who was quite well versed in the history of the mine, commented, 'That was the year Tudor Morgan went into partnership with my grandfather.'

'It was also the year the engine house, the one that's no longer in use, was built,' Rhys said.

She was about to ask him why that was of interest to him when Jessica put in, 'I haven't told you my good news yet, Meredith.' As she spoke she led the way into the porch. 'I'm starting work tomorrow as Rhys's PA.'

'Congratulations.' She felt, before she could check or analyse it, the oddest pang of envy.

'Thanks,' Jessica replied. She slanted a smile up at Rhys. 'I know I'm going to find working for my new boss very stimulating.'

Margred was crossing the hall with a vase of pink carnations for the drawing-room.

'Hello, it's nice to see you, Rhys,' she greeted him with a smile. 'I was about to make tea. Can I offer you a cup?'

'No, thanks, Margred,' he replied. As he was speaking Meredith found herself noting the ruthless line of his jaw, the devilish cleft in his chin, his firm lips. 'I've only called for a minute to collect some photos.'

As if he sensed he was being scrutinised, his cobalt eyes alighted on Meredith. She intended to look away quickly, but his speculative gaze was like a challenge and for an instant she couldn't break free from the compulsion to return it.

Electricity seemed to flicker like a raw flame along her nerves and, feeling herself blush, she said the first words that came into her head. 'I think the album's in the study.'

'Let's go in search of it, then,' Jessica said.

She and Rhys walked off down the hall while Meredith was glad to go into the drawing-room. She wasn't the least attracted to Rhys, she insisted, and yet there was no denying that something simmered between them not far beneath the surface. She told herself, as she had done on other occasions, to ignore it.

Margred set the vase of flowers down on the grand piano. 'So Rhys gave you a lift home,' she commented. 'Was that by accident or design?'

'It was very much by accident.'

'He makes you angry a lot of the time, doesn't he?' the housekeeper observed.

Had Meredith seen the knowing light in her eyes she would certainly have challenged it. Instead she gave a short frustrated sigh.

'I don't know why I let him rub me up the wrong way,' she said.

'He has a very forceful personality.'

'He's also unbearably mocking,' Meredith said, commenting, 'Not that Jessica seems to find him so. Did you know she's going to work for him?'

'I wonder how long she'll like that,' Margred said. 'She'll have to get up early for a change.'

'Jessica knows all about the company, having worked for it before, and she's very efficient.'

'At some things,' Margred agreed. She brought one of the large double blooms forward. 'Especially at hitching her wagon to a rising star.'

Meredith shot her a questioning look.

'You're not suggesting . . .?' she began, certain she couldn't have understood what the housekeeper seemed to be implying.

'Yes, I am,' Margred confirmed calmly. 'To my mind Jessica's always had an eye to the main chance. Rhys is rich and successful. She may well have decided that, after a decent interval, she'd like to marry him.'

'I've never heard of anything so ridiculous!' Meredith said with an indignant laugh. 'Stephen hasn't been dead six months yet!'

'I'm not saying she wasn't fond of your brother,' the housekeeper answered, 'but Jessica's always been, in my opinion, rather a shallow person. I don't think she's got it in her to grieve for anyone for very long.'

For some reason the idea of Rhys becoming linked romantically with Jessica awoke a demon alarmingly akin to jealousy in Meredith's heart.

At that moment her sister-in-law came into the drawing-room. She went straight to the window seat and said laughingly, 'Honestly, Meredith! Sending us on a wild-goose chase! No wonder we couldn't find the album. It was here all the time.'

CHAPTER SEVEN

THE Sunday paper tucked under her arm, Meredith wandered out of the drawing-room on to the patio. The sky was a deep brilliant blue. In the distance the mountains that were laced with the indigo of heather were magnificent in the sunlight.

Wrought-iron garden furniture was set out to capitalise on the view of lawns and rose-garden. Jet lay in the circle of shade under the white table, his muzzle resting on his front paws. He pricked up his ears as he heard Meredith's step, wagged his tail lazily and then settled down again as she draped her brightly patterned overshirt over the back of a nearby chair.

The tropical print in blues and greens matched her bikini with its halter-tie bandeau top and ruched briefs. She smoothed suntan lotion on to her arms and then sat down on a comfortable lounger to finish oiling herself lavishly.

Fair-skinned, she had to take care she didn't burn, and she untied the halter straps of her bikini top so as not to get lotion on them. She left the straps hanging loose to avoid strap marks as she tanned, and then reached for the colour magazine which came with the Sunday paper and began to read.

'I thought I'd drive to the beach for a swim. Do you want to come?' a female voice asked some while later.

Meredith glanced up. Absorbed in an article on the wines of Burgundy, she hadn't heard Jessica approach. She tossed the magazine aside and stretched like a cat.

'Good idea!' she agreed readily, adding immediately afterwards, 'Oh, wait a minute, what time is it?'

'Ten past three,' Jessica answered. 'Why?'

'I've got a pupil coming for a music lesson at four,' Meredith explained. 'I'd forgotten for a moment.'

'Well, that answers that.'

'We could go to the beach later,' Meredith suggested.

Her sister-in-law strolled over to the balustrade and stood admiring the gardens and the mountains beyond. The white crinkle fabric sundress she was wearing fell in romantic lines, emphasising her willowy gracefulness.

'We could,' she replied, 'but I've got plans for this evening. I want to drop a report round to Rhys.'

'Won't it wait till tomorrow?'

'He's not in the office tomorrow,' Jessica answered. She turned back as she mocked, 'Enjoy giving your music lesson. I'm off now for a swim.'

'OK, see you later,' Meredith laughed as she picked up her magazine.

The heat made her feel pleasantly sleepy and a few moments later she closed her eyes, enjoying the sun's warmth on her bare skin. Around her were the lazy sounds of summer, the calling of a song thrush and the intermittent buzzing of the bees from the flower borders.

Soon her thoughts began to eddy. It was the sound of a man's step on the terrace which roused her from sleep. She sighed drowsily as someone leant over her. The next instant lips that were warm and firm brushed hers in a feather-light kiss.

Her heart seemed to lurch in wonder. A soft sound of pleasure escaped her and then was lost as the warm lips returned to hers, evoking a response from her that was as sweet as it was willing.

A hand stroked her waist, sending delicious shivers over her skin. Her dark fringe of lashes were curved against her cheek. In all the times Trefor had kissed her it had never been so drugging and so heady, a promise of pleasures yet to come.

Their embrace seemed to go on for ever, and when finally it ended she opened her eyes slowly, a misty glow in their depths. But her gaze wasn't met, as she'd expected, by Trefor's. It was met by Rhys's. As if a bucket of cold water had been thrown over her, she jerked into a sitting position.

For an instant she stared at him gasping, unable to believe that he had been the one to kiss her. He was watching her enigmatically, a faintly sensual quirk to his mouth.

Her dazed senses took in his casual attire. He was wearing jeans and a cream short-sleeved shirt which was open at the throat revealing the dark hairs that curled against his tanned skin. His jeans fitted snugly, emphasising his aggressive masculinity.

There was a faint tinge of colour along his cheekbones in the aftermath of their passion, but his voice was lazy and amused as ever as he said, 'If you're going to kiss me like that I'll have to call round more often.'

His mockery shattered her stunned bewilderment. Fury sparked in her amber eyes.

'How...how dare you?' she spluttered, finding her voice at last. 'How dare you sneak up on me, pretending to be Trefor?'

'Do you kiss him with such warmth and abandon?'

As Rhys spoke his gaze made a leisurely appraisal of her, admiring the curve of her long legs and the full swell of her breasts. She blushed hotly as she realised that her halter straps hung loose, and hurriedly tied them behind her neck.

Swinging her feet on to the sun-warmed paving stones, she stood up. Clad only in her bikini, she felt very naked.

'How did you get in?' she asked, her voice unsteady with temper.

'When I rang the bell there was no answer,' he told her. His black hair gleamed like polished jet in the sunlight as he got to his feet. 'On the off-chance you might be in the garden this lovely sunny afternoon I came round the side.'

'Then you can leave by the same route!' she told him.

Rhys ignored her clipped command. 'Your father's playing golf this afternoon. It's

Margred's day off, I imagine, and Jessica's car is gone. Does this mean we're alone, the two of us?' he asked lazily.

She tossed her head back, trying her hardest to conceal the fact that her heart was thumping erratically. Until Rhys had appeared the afternoon had seemed lazy and peaceful. Now the very air was tingling.

'I have a pupil coming for a lesson.' It was twenty minutes at the most since she'd asked Jessica the time, but she added, 'I'm expecting her at any moment.'

'Dressed like that?' Rhys mocked, caressing her figure with his masculine gaze.

'Must I spell it out for you?' she breathed angrily. 'I want you to leave!'

'I've only just arrived,' he pointed out, broad shoulders hunching in a slight shrug.

He was goading her, exactly as he had ever since she'd had the misfortune to meet him. She could feel her temper deserting her, but held on to it with an effort, instinct warning her that not to do so would be somehow to play into his hands.

'Very well,' she said tightly. 'Since you won't do as I ask, you can sit out here on your own. I'm going indoors!'

Her green and blue bikini was daring. Hating the idea of his blatant masculine gaze staring after her as she turned her back on him and walked to the house, she went towards the chair where her overshirt lay. Rhys, who was standing closer to the chair than she was, anticipated what she was after. He picked her overshirt up before she had the chance to claim it.

Certain he meant to tease her, she demanded, 'Give me that!'

To her surprise he acquiesced.

'You know, this is the first time I've seen you so rattled,' he observed, lazy amusement in his voice as twice her arm missed the left sleeve before she managed to shrug the overshirt on. 'That kiss of ours really shook you, didn't it?'

'What shook me,' she said, infuriated that he had hit on the truth, 'was your outstanding nerve!'

It would have been sensible to have retreated into the house. But it seemed that the tension which linked them was such that she could no more stop herself from rising to his remarks than he could refrain from making them.

Flicking a strand of burnished hair over her shoulder, she went on, 'You knew perfectly well I thought you were Trefor and you took advantage of me!'

'So when are you going to give him your answer?' Rhys enquired.

'Trefor hasn't set a deadline,' she said.

'Why are you keeping him waiting?'

'Because...' she began, and then fell silent. She had almost admitted that what had happened at Rhys's house still haunted her.

'Go on?' Rhys drawled.

'Why all the interest?' she asked defensively.

'Are you trying to work out whether or not I want you for myself?' Rhys mocked.

Her temper began to flare at his arrogance. 'I'm not so conceited!' she sparked. 'You've made it very clear you enjoy getting a rise out of me. If you wanted me in any way that was meaningful you'd take me seriously!'

'You're a fool, Meredith.'

The curtness of his tone made her glance at him sharply. A hint of impatience was etched into his strikingly masculine features. She was aware of his advantage over her in height, and of the width of his shoulders. She was equally aware that the more they sparred, the more volatile the atmosphere seemed to become.

'What makes you say I'm a fool?' she asked, her chin tilting.

His gaze narrowed on her, a glint that might have been anger in his cobalt eyes. 'If you were the least bit clued up about yourself you wouldn't need to ask.'

'While you, of course, are absolutely clued up about me,' she said. Though she spoke sarcastically her heart was beginning to thump.

'I had you fathomed the first time I looked into those fascinating amber eyes of yours,' Rhys answered.

Merely to return his gaze was to feel a flush of sexual awareness. She clenched her hands, the effect their conversation and his virility were having on her pulse-rate adding to her temper and her confusion.

'Are you making a pass at me?' she asked.

'Would you like me to?' he mocked.

'No, I wouldn't like! Give up, Rhys. All the other women you've known may have fallen at your feet, but I'm not going to.' Something flickered across the hard planes of his face and, suddenly, she was convinced that with her shot in the dark she was right. 'That's what this is all about, isn't it?' she exclaimed. 'You hoped I was going to find you irresistible and you simply can't get over the fact that I'm completely indifferent to you!'

'Is that a fact?' he said. Taking hold of her by the forearms, he pulled her none too gently to his chest.

'Let go of me!' she demanded.

'Why, you're trembling!' he exclaimed softly, husky laughter edging his words. 'The last time you trembled in my arms was when we danced together. That could have been nerves because Trefor was watching you, but now we're alone together.'

'You don't need to remind me,' she said breathlessly.

'I'm surprised it bothers you,' he mocked. 'Didn't you just say you're totally indifferent to me?'

'I…I'm not indifferent. I actively dislike you!' she flashed breathlessly, trying to free herself. 'You're arrogant and conceited and you think every woman is longing to have an affair with you!'

'If your luck holds you just might be one of them,' he said.

A torrent of angry words tumbled through her mind. What stopped her from hurling them at him was his closeness. He would only have to bend his head for his mouth to claim hers. The prospect made a hot shiver trace over her skin.

As if amused by her mutinous silence, Rhys released her. His tone ironic, he said, 'Would you tell Jessica I found the photograph album she lent me very useful? I hate to disillusion you when you obviously think I called round on the off-chance of finding you alone, but I came to return it.'

It lay on the wrought-iron table where he must have placed it when he'd strolled on to the patio. She noticed it for the first time as he drew her attention to it.

With that he walked away, tall, broad-shouldered, virility stamped into every line of him. Infuriated by his mockery and his conceit, she snatched up the album, meaning to hurl it after him.

Yet somehow she didn't dare. The tension between her and Rhys needed defusing. It would be folly to ignite it. Her totally uncharacteristic lack of courage adding to the storm of emotion inside her, she slapped the album of old photographs of the mine back on the table.

She drew an angry breath. Her legs were trembling rather strangely and she could still feel the warm seductive pressure of Rhys's mouth on hers. She pressed the back of her hand to her lips to erase the disturbing sensation, but it was not as easy to erase the man himself from her mind.

She had calmed down a little by the time she had changed and her pupil had arrived, but the events of the afternoon made it hard for her to concentrate on the music lesson she was giving. She kept going over what had happened.

Rhys was experienced and his technique was excellent. She tried to explain away her response by telling herself that she had responded to him for a few seconds as any woman would. And yet she could not forget the desire which had heated her blood, the sweet longing to give and give of herself, a longing different from anything she had ever felt before.

Her fingers went unconsciously to her lips as she tried to bring order to her inner confusion. The conclusion she came to was that she needed to talk to Rhys. It needed courage, but the only thing to do was to beard the lion in his den.

She would call on Rhys and tell him to stay away from her in future. His interest in her was purely predatory and she could imagine only too well the heartbreak of being caught up in a transitory whirlwind affair with him.

'It's rather late to be visiting, isn't it?' her father commented when she walked into the drawing-room to say she was going out.

'I'm delivering a message to someone,' she said. 'It won't take me long.'

Gerallt picked up the remote control switch and lowered the volume of the television.

'Before you go,' he said. 'I noticed Jessica seemed rather on edge and short-tempered this evening. I wondered if you knew what was wrong.'

Meredith shook her head. She too had noticed that Jessica was very snappy. The only explanation she could offer was, 'Perhaps she's finding she's taken on more than she bargained for with her new job. Did you know she drove over to Rhys's specially with a report earlier on?'

'No, I didn't.'

'If she expected him to be appreciative I imagine she was disappointed,' Meredith said, her eyes smouldering as they invariably did whenever she thought of her antagonist. 'I doubt whether "thank you" is in his vocabulary.'

Her remark caused her father to arch an eyebrow in her direction. 'That's rather uncalled for, don't you think?' he said.

From his point of view perhaps it was, but from her own Rhys took without asking. Resentment against him sharpened her tongue as she thought once again of the long drugging kiss he had stolen that afternoon, the way he had touched her.

'He's about as gentlemanly as a buccaneer! Perhaps his ancestors were Cornish wreckers!'

Her father was amused. 'It sounds as if you're harbouring romantic notions about the man,' he said.

'Well, I can assure you I'm not,' Meredith answered.

Vaguely provoked by her father's amused comment, she left the room, her skirt swaying.

The pale blue of dusk had given way to the darker tones of evening and she switched from side-lights to headlights as she drove towards Bryn Uchel. Every now and then a twist or a bend in the road revealed the magnificent expanse of the river, which lay like a polished sheet of pewter, reflecting the shadowy mountains.

It wasn't until she came to the outskirts of the town that she realised to her concern that, having come this far, she didn't know exactly how she was going to say what she had to put to Rhys. She could imagine his sardonic smile as he listened to her. Quite possibly he would jump to the conclusion that her real reason for calling was because she was drawn to him as to a magnet.

Suddenly she had cold feet. It was very late to be calling on a man who made her so aware of her femininity. She felt she needed a chaperon but what she had to say to Rhys was for his ears alone.

Instead of taking the road to Glan-wern she turned left, taking the road which wound steeply up the side of the valley, needing to collect her thoughts. Near the top of the hill she drew in by the side of the road. She turned off the ignition and sat for a moment enveloped in silence and darkness.

Then, restlessly, she threw open her door and got out of the car. The rough grass verge gave way to a weathered slab wall. Leaning against it, she looked over the darkened fields that sloped away into the distance towards the lights which twinkled on the other side of the valley.

When she thought clearly she knew it would be impossible to stop seeing Rhys. He and her father were in business together and it was inevitable he would come to the house periodically. It would be better perhaps to say nothing but to be distant and frosty in his company.

Her reasons for changing her mind about calling on him were sound and ones she would have been happy with had she been able to forget the willingness with which she had responded to his embrace that afternoon. And then there was that time at his house . . .

Stop it, an inner voice demanded, cutting the playback of memory short. She forced herself to drink in the tranquillity of the warm summer night.

The lofty dark sky overhead was studded with stars. Beneath it were the resting fields with their sleeping flocks, the friendly lights of the town in the distance and the vastness of the mountains which stretched for miles all around. She drew a long deep breath and then once more she returned to her car and drove back the way she had come to Pencarreg Hall.

'I've got a lot to see to today but I wonder if I should take the afternoon off to make sure I'm home when Mari and Dan arrive,' Gerallt said that Friday at breakfast, speaking of his sister and her husband.

'I'll be home from school at four,' Meredith reminded him, 'although I don't expect they'll get here much before six.'

'They said they weren't going to get on the road too early,' her father commented on their phone call the night before. 'I think it was very sensible of them to arrange to stay overnight at Heathrow before picking up the car. It will mean they won't be too tired when they get here.'

'It takes a while to catch up with jet lag,' Meredith agreed.

Gerallt glanced at his watch and then frowned. 'Where's Jessica got to this morning? I want to be off in a few minutes.'

'I'll go and give her a shout,' Meredith volunteered, setting down her coffee-cup.

She ran upstairs and tapped on her sister-in-law's bedroom door.

'Come in,' a muffled voice called.

Meredith popped her head round the door to see that Jessica had only just got out of bed. In a pale blue jacquard silk nightgown she looked the picture of slim elegance. Thinking that her sister-in-law had overslept, Meredith began, 'You'd better hurry, Jessica. Dad wants to be off very shortly. As soon as he finishes his breakfast he'll be pacing up and down.'

'Tell him I shan't need a lift this morning,' came the reply. 'I'm not going into work today. I've got a migraine.'

'Oh, I'm sorry,' Meredith said. 'Can I get you anything?'

'A cup of tea would be nice.'

'I'll ask Margred to bring you one up.'

Jessica sighed. 'Thanks,' she said, rubbing her temples. 'I hope Rhys can manage without me for the day. I've given him a call to explain.'

'He isn't at work already, is he?' Meredith asked, surprised.

'He likes to get in early,' came the reply.

It was no wonder her father was impressed with him, she thought. Gerallt admired single-mindedness and energy.

'He's a very exciting man to work for,' her sister-in-law went on. 'Getting the job as his PA has been a real shot in the arm for me.'

Her inflexion as much as her words made what Margred had said the other day flash into Meredith's mind. She didn't believe for one moment that her sister-in-law was setting her cap at Rhys. But it was possible that without realising it she was becoming involved with him.

'You're not falling for the mocking devil, are you, Jessica?' she said in concern.

Her sister-in-law glanced sharply at her before going over to her dressing-table to pick up the photograph of Stephen which stood on it. She gazed at it for a moment and then set it down again.

Meredith's heart contracted. Reproaching herself for reminding her sister-in-law and wishing she hadn't spoken, she said quickly, 'I didn't mean... I was only trying to warn you. I know how lonely you must feel at times and I have a hunch Rhys is the sort of man who might take advantage of that.'

'Go on,' Jessica prompted coolly.

'I don't want to see you get hurt,' Meredith said, 'and I think working with Rhys you could be.'

Her sister-in-law tilted her head on one side. 'Are you sure you're warning me, or are you warning me off?' she said.

Startled by the accusation, Meredith protested, 'No, of course not!'

'It sounds to me very much as if you are,' Jessica said, her blue eyes hostile. 'Perhaps I should ask you the very question you've just asked me. Have you fallen for him yourself?'

'Don't be so ridiculous!' Meredith exclaimed with a protesting laugh.

Jessica studied her coolly. 'Rhys is a good catch and he seems to find your charm appealing,' she said, 'but, just the same, I wouldn't start angling for him if I were you.'

'For heaven's sake!' Meredith exclaimed. 'I don't even like Rhys. My instincts tell me he's dangerous.'

'And what do your instincts tell you about Trefor?' Jessica sneered sweetly. 'Not much, presumably.'

'What do you mean?' Meredith said.

Jessica seemed to debate her answer for a moment. Then she said with a flash of malice, 'He's not quite the open, honest character you seem to think he is. At least, I assume he hasn't told you.'

Meredith threw her a mystified look. 'Told me what?' she said.

'I suggest you ask him,' her sister-in-law replied with a little shrug. 'And if he won't tell you, maybe I will.'

Gerallt's voice interrupted their conversation. 'Am I going to be kept waiting all day?' he boomed from the foot of the stairs.

'I do wish he wouldn't shout,' Jessica winced, her hand going to her temples.

'I'd better tell Dad you're staying in bed this morning.'

Puzzled, and vaguely uneasy, Meredith ran downstairs and passed on Jessica's message.

'It took her long enough to explain,' her father frowned.

'We got talking about other things.'

'So I've been standing here waiting while you two have been gossiping!' Gerallt said shortly.

'Now, Dad, the office won't fall apart just because you're a couple of minutes late,' Meredith teased.

His face relaxed, a glimmer of humour appearing in his steely grey eyes. 'I suppose I do get a bit grumpy when other people keep me waiting,' he conceded.

'Just a little,' she said laughingly. She reached up and planted a kiss on his cheek. 'I must hurry, too. See you this evening.'

CHAPTER EIGHT

MEREDITH walked across the school hall. In her arms was a box full of castanets, cymbals and triangles. Beside her, very pleased to be helping, trotted one of her eight-year-olds, an engaging little girl who chattered on as ceaselessly as a babbling brook.

'Mummy says I've got on so well with the recorder she wants me to start piano lessons.'

'That's nice, Nia,' Meredith answered. 'Have you got a piano at home?'

'Yes. My Daddy plays for me sometimes, but he plays a lot of wrong notes.'

'Does he?' Meredith said, amused. She unlocked the music cupboard and slid the box she was carrying on to one of the shelves. 'The music books go in the corner,' she told the little girl.

Nia set them down in a neat pile and then remarked, 'I like it best when I play the tambourine or the drums.'

'Let's see,' Meredith mused, quick to understand what the little girl was getting at, 'You had a triangle this week and last week, and before that...'

'I had the bells,' Nia reminded her.

'So you did. Well, then, next lesson it must be your turn for one of the tambourines.' As Nia's face lit up she laughed. 'Run along now, or you'll miss all your play.'

As the little girl went off happily, Meredith locked the music cupboard. The sunlight was flooding in through the long windows, casting gleaming oblongs on the wood block floor, while outside came the shouts and cries of the children in the playground.

Usually she spent the lunch-hour on the premises but today she decided to call in at the hospital to see Trefor. She wouldn't admit that she felt strangely uneasy, but Jessica's words had come to mind several times that morning and she found herself trying to fathom them once again as she drove into the hospital car park.

She pushed through the double set of swing doors and was heading for the reception desk when Trefor stepped out of one of the lifts.

'Hello,' he said with a warm smile, slipping his stethoscope into the pocket of his white coat. 'This is unexpected. You've been rather elusive lately. What brings you here?'

'I wanted to talk to you,' she said. 'Have you got a minute?'

'I was about to go to lunch, so yes,' he answered. 'I've got a surprise for you. Why don't we stroll over to the cafeteria together?'

She checked her watch. 'I haven't really got time to stop for lunch,' she said. 'I mustn't be late back.'

'Then let's go into the gardens and you can tell me what's on your mind.'

The hospital grounds were well-tended. Neat flower borders and smooth green lawns softened the angles of the buildings and gave pleasant views from the wards. They found a seat near a silver fir and sat down.

'Now let me guess,' Trefor teased as he stretched out his legs and draped his arm along the back of the seat. 'You want to know if I'm working this weekend or not.'

'No, it's not that,' she said. 'I just need you to throw some light on something Jessica said to me this morning.'

Something flickered for an instant across Trefor's face. 'What's that?' he asked.

'She said there was something you hadn't told me and that I ought to ask you what it was.'

'I can't think what she meant,' he hedged.

'She said she'd tell me if you wouldn't,' Meredith said.

Trefor's jawline hardened. 'The little bitch!' he muttered angrily. 'I should have guessed she'd be spiteful enough to do something like this.'

A sense of apprehension made Meredith's heart start to thump.

'Do something like what?' she asked.

Trefor's eyes flickered to meet hers. Reluctantly he said, 'I didn't want you to know, but it seems thanks to Jessica you'll have to. We…we were lovers for a time.'

The colour left Meredith's face. 'You were what?' she breathed.

'For weeks she'd been giving me these cool yet smouldering glances,' Trefor mumbled. 'I wanted to ignore them. I wanted to ignore her, but then last Christmas——'

'You mean Stephen was still alive!' Meredith cut in. A storm of emotion blazed up inside her, taking over from the initial stupefying shock. 'You took his wife!'

'I know you're angry and upset, but I swear it didn't mean anything.'

'It didn't mean anything!' she repeated, stumbling to her feet. 'You cheated on me! You slept with my sister-in-law, and you say it doesn't mean anything!'

'Meredith, for pity's sake!' he snapped. 'Will you stop being so dramatic? I'm not proud of what happened. I've regretted it ever since, but I've said I'm sorry——'

'Do you think sorry puts it right?' she cried, her voice breaking with outrage.

'I've agreed,' he said, losing patience, 'it should never have happened, but fidelity means different things to different people, and I don't see I need to go down on my knees to you because I had a brief fling with your sister-in-law!'

She stared at him in disbelief. Fidelity to her was the cornerstone of a relationship. He didn't seem to realise he had betrayed her. Angrily, she said, 'I don't ever want to see you again.'

'You'll have to or look a complete fool.' Trefor was angry too.

She threw off the hand he laid on her arm. 'I've finished with you!'

'Then wait until you've seen *The Times* tomorrow. I've put our engagement in it.'

'You've what?' she breathed.

'I've just announced our engagement in *The Times*,' Trefor snapped.

'You had no right!' she burst out. 'How dare you when I never said I'd marry you?'

'I dared because I wasn't having you turn me down,' Trefor said, his face set hard. 'And what's more you can't now, not unless you don't mind people thinking you put the announcement in and I've jilted you, because that's what everyone will think.'

'I don't give a damn what they think!' she cried.

Angrily she turned on her heel, breaking into a run because she couldn't get away from him fast enough.

Pride got her through the afternoon at school. She was afraid to let herself think lest she broke down in tears. Instead she carried on as if there was nothing wrong, while inside she was an unexploded bomb of fury and betrayal.

She was thankful when the last bell of the afternoon rang. As she walked to her car, suddenly she desperately needed someone to talk to. Switching on the ignition, she made up her mind to drive up the valley to the mine to see her father.

The stretch of road from Bryn Uchel to the Mynydd-y-Glyn mine was one of her favourites, but today she hardly seemed to notice the red oaks which clothed the sturdy shoulders of the mountains, or the way the sunlight slanted through the branches of the fir trees. Her lower lip trembled as she remembered the hospital grounds, Trefor saying he'd had an affair with Jessica. How could he? she kept thinking. How could he?

High up on the hillside slips of scree pierced the forest, marking the mysterious mouths of adits, long since abandoned. Nature had reclaimed most of the old workings, but the chimney stack of the Cornish engine house could still be glimpsed among the trees as she slowed for the mine gates.

The security guard, recognising her car, waved her through and she turned in, followed by a heavy truck which soon veered off towards the open-cast workings. There was plenty of space to park in front of the main building, and she drew to a halt and got out.

A short flight of steps marked the entrance to the clerical department. She crossed the reception area with its resilient plush carpeting and bursts of greenery and went through the double doors to her father's office.

Gerallt's secretary, a pleasant middle-aged woman, glanced up from her typewriter as she walked into the outer office.

'Hello, Meredith,' she said with friendly surprise. 'We don't often see you here.'

'I . . . I wanted a word with Dad,' Meredith explained. 'Is he busy at the moment?'

'He's gone to inspect the Llech-faen pumping engine with one of the safety officers, but he should be back soon. Would you like to go into his office and wait?' she said, standing up to open the door.

Meredith forced herself to smile her thanks as she went inside. The door closed behind her with a click. She wandered aimlessly towards the windows and stared out at the road and the valley beyond. She had been forced to put on an act all afternoon and it was a relief to find herself alone.

As she stood there tears suddenly brimmed in her eyes. Since lunchtime the anger she had felt had changed. In its place instead was a painful ache of disillusionment. How could she have been so naïve? Why had she never realised that Trefor was carrying a torch for her sister-in-law? Lord, the deception hurt!

Her head lifted as she heard the sound of the door opening. She turned, thinking it was her father, and saw to her dismay that Rhys had walked in, tall and arrestingly masculine. His well-cut jacket was open on a navy silk tie and light-blue shirt that enhanced his attractive swarthiness.

He stopped dead as he saw her. The stern lines of his face registered a frown of concern as he noted her shimmering eyes. 'Meredith, what's wrong?' he asked.

She struggled to pull herself together. Fumbling in her sleeve for a handkerchief, she said, 'N... nothing.'

Footsteps brought him closer.

'Don't give me nothing,' he answered. A firm hand dropped on her shoulder and her chin was tilted up for her smarting eyes to meet the scrutiny of his gaze. 'You've been crying, if I'm not mistaken. What's happened?'

'Nothing,' she insisted and then, to her dismay, her voice broke and she burst into tears again.

With a smothered exclamation Rhys pulled her into his arms. Her feeble attempt at resistance was overridden as he wrapped her to him. There was no escaping from his embrace and, as his masculine gentleness shattered her defences, she turned her cheek into the hardness of his shoulder.

Rhys stroked her hair, murmuring soothing words while she wept helplessly. His arms were like a haven, strong and comforting. It was only as she steadied that the musky male fragrance of his aftershave began to disturb her senses. The iron feel of him not only reassured, it sent a tiny shiver down her spine.

Before the confusing sensations could grow stronger, she gathered herself together and raised her head.

'I . . . didn't mean to burst into tears,' she said, her voice catching on a little sob. 'I . . . I'm sorry.'

'Don't be silly,' he answered, his voice kind.

She gave him the glimmer of a rueful smile, unaware that her amber eyes, which shone with tears, enhanced the loveliness of her face, or that there was in her faltering smile a vulnerability which Rhys had never seen before. She only knew that, as he looked down at her, the mood of their embrace underwent a swift change.

A dark intensity smouldered in his gaze and she gave a little gasp as his fingers tightened on her shoulders. One instant he was drawing her towards him, the next he had released her so abruptly that she staggered a little.

'Rhys . . . what . . . what's wrong?' she gulped, unable to understand why he had let her go in such a sudden fashion.

'That's what you're going to tell me,' he answered.

A large sofa in red leather was shaped to fit the corner of her father's office. In charge of the situation as always, Rhys led her over to it and sat down beside her. Her tears had left her feeling shaky and she sat staring at her clenched fingers, not knowing how to begin.

Rhys reached for her hand. Gently he said, 'Is it as bad as all...?' He broke off, and as her eyes went to his face she saw his brows were drawn together. His expression hawkish and keen, he demanded, 'Where's your slave bracelet?'

The local jeweller had snapped it undone for her when she had called in earlier that week and explained the catch had broken. He'd told her the bracelet wasn't worth repairing and she hadn't been sorry to leave it on the counter.

'Well?' Rhys insisted.

She was aware of a strange tension in the air which, like a hot dry wind, seemed suddenly to appear from nowhere. It seemed to threaten her, making her hostility come surging back.

'I've finished with Trefor,' she said. Her eyes began to spark as she remembered Rhys's gibes at her. 'No doubt you're pleased to be proved right. You said I was a fool to go chasing after Trefor.'

'You didn't chase him,' Rhys answered curtly, 'and I'm not pleased you're hurt.'

His answer took her by surprise, cutting the ground from under her. Bewildered, she faltered, 'If you didn't think I was chasing Trefor...then why...why did you say I was?'

'I knew it needled you,' Rhys answered.

'Why did you want to needle me?' Meredith wanted to know.

'Why did you start an argument with me every time a sense of rapport started to build between us?' he returned.

She could have denied the charge, only it wasn't a moment for evasion or half-truths.

'I don't know,' she whispered honestly.

The masculine line of Rhys's mouth twisted in a rather mirthless smile. 'Evidently not,' he said under his breath as he put his arm around her and drew her against him.

She leaned her head against his shoulder. Out of all the people in the world Rhys was the very last she would have chosen to run to with her troubles, yet here she was nestling close to him. The all important defences she had built up against him lay in ruins and strangely their destruction didn't even seem to matter.

'Oh, Rhys, how could he have done it?' she whispered.

'Done what?'

She swallowed hard. 'S . . . slept with . . . with someone else.' She couldn't bear to name her sister-in-law. It was too sordid. In a rush of unhappiness she went on, telling him what before she had refused to tell. 'I knew in my heart at Derec's party that he and I weren't right for each other, but what I found out today was so disillusioning!'

'It won't seem so bad in time,' Rhys said in a kindly way.

She bit her lip. He was right, but she couldn't take comfort in his words because of the storm which, thanks to Trefor, was going to break tomorrow.

'I know, but what makes it so bad...' she whispered.

'Go on,' he prompted.

'Trefor's put our engagement in tomorrow's paper. I'm staggered he could think of such a thing when I hadn't said yes. It will be all over town tomorrow and, to make matters worse, my aunt and uncle flew into Heathrow yesterday. They're arriving this evening to stay with us. Now I'll have to explain to them...'

'He's really landed you in it, hasn't he?' Rhys said as she trailed off miserably. 'Would you like some help in getting out of it?'

'But...how?' she asked.

'Let's start with you inviting me to dinner this evening.'

'OK.' She couldn't see how it was going to help but she agreed.

'Don't say anything to anyone. Leave it all to me.'

'You know, you're so much nicer than...' she began and then broke off, blushing painfully as she realised how tactless she was being.

Amusement flickered across Rhys's chiselled features. 'Coming from you, that remark's quite an accolade,' he mocked. 'What time shall I come round?'

She got to her feet. 'Is...is six o'clock too early?'

'Six is fine,' he agreed. He handed her his handkerchief. 'Before you go, your mascara's run,' he said.

She rubbed her face with the pristine hand-kerchief. There was no mirror in the office for her to check on her appearance and she asked, 'Is that better?'

'You look a little less like a waif,' he said, a glimmer of a smile in his eyes.

Waiflike was how she felt. Instinct told her that Rhys was used to sophisticated women, the sort who would remain beautiful and sophisticated even when they cried.

He walked with her back to Reception. Still shaken by the turn of events, she was very quiet. It wasn't until they drew to a halt by the heavy glass doors that, with an effort, she pulled herself together.

'Rhys, I...I really appreciate your saying you'll come over this evening,' she told him, trying hard to keep her voice steady. 'You've been very kind altogether.'

'That's what friends are for,' he said, dismissing her gratitude.

She looked into his strong, masculine face. As her gaze met his, she felt her pulse flutter. It was a sensation which was familiar and one which had always prompted her to hostility before. Now, obeying an impulse, she reached up and kissed him.

'Thanks,' she whispered. With that she turned and went out through the swing doors. She was aware that her heart was beating rather erratically without knowing the cause. She did not glance back. Had she done, she would have seen Rhys staring after her thoughtfully while his lean fingers rubbed the slight roughness of his cheek which had been grazed by her lips.

She arrived back home and, her eyes full of sparks, she marched into the drawing-room. It was empty. She had expected to find Jessica there. Intent on finding and confronting her sister-in-law, she pivoted and went upstairs.

She met Margred on the landing as she drew level with Jessica's bedroom door.

'You're home later than usual,' the housekeeper remarked. 'Did you stay to fit in another rehearsal for the concert?'

'I stopped off at the mine,' Meredith explained.

Margred gave her a probing glance.

'Is everything all right?' she asked. 'You look upset.'

'I...I've had a rotten day,' Meredith said, and thought that tomorrow was going to rival it.

'How about a cup of tea?' the housekeeper suggested sympathetically.

'Thanks, Margred, but I...I want to have a word with Jessica.'

'She's not in her room. She's gone for a walk,' the housekeeper told her. 'I think she hoped it might help to clear her migraine.'

'I'll catch her later,' Meredith said tonelessly.

She realised suddenly that she had been using her anger against Jessica to ease all the tension inside her. And if it weren't for Rhys she'd be feeling even worse.

The ache beneath her ribs eased a little as she remembered how surprisingly understanding he had been. It seemed she was no judge of men at all, she thought as she sat on her bed. Not only had she been wrong about Trefor, but she'd also been wrong, though in a different way, about Rhys.

She felt as if she was seeing him for the first time. His mockery and the ruthlessness she sensed in him had meant she'd overlooked his other qualities. Or maybe she'd been afraid to see them, something inside her said. The flash of perception seemed to make no sense and, in no fit state to analyse her feelings, she abandoned the thought.

She decided what to change into for the evening and then took a shower. The hot pelting water that streamed over her skin was therapeutic and she let her mind go blank as she shampooed her hair. In a while she would have to think what she was going to tell not just her family but everyone who would learn about her engagement in tomorrow's paper.

In her bedroom she made-up with her usual care. Then she slipped on a very feminine turquoise dress that enhanced the burnished beauty of her hair and gave her fair skin a translucent glow. Pretty high-heeled sandals completed her outfit.

With her slim shoulders squared, she went downstairs to see if Margred needed any help. She paused on the last stair, hearing the murmur of voices from the drawing-room. Her eyes began to smoulder as she heard Jessica's languid voice intermingled with the bass tones of her father's.

'Hello, Meredith,' Gerallt said, glimpsing her through the open door as she crossed the hall.

'Hi, Dad.'

With little option to do otherwise, she entered the drawing-room. There was so much anger inside her that she didn't trust herself to glance in Jessica's direction. She was afraid that if her eyes collided with her sister-in-law's deceptively guileless gaze her self-control and her temper would snap.

'I understand you called in at the mine earlier,' her father remarked.

'Yes, I...I asked Rhys to join us for dinner.'

'How nice!' Jessica purred.

It was on the tip of Meredith's tongue to ask acidly if Jessica intended making a set for Rhys in the same way that she'd made a set for her ex-boyfriend. She bit back the barbed question as Gerallt teased, 'Does this mean you and Rhys have called a truce at last?'

'Yes, it does,' she agreed.

The crunch of a car drawing up on the gravel outside saved her from saying anything more. Rising from his chair, Gerallt announced, 'That must be Mari and Dan.' He caught sight of the dark-green Volvo that had pulled up in front of the porch and said delightedly, 'Yes, it's them!'

Pushing open the french windows, he strode outside to greet his sister and her husband. Meredith followed him down the steps, her face lighting up as she saw her aunt and uncle getting out of their hired car. Beyond them she glimpsed Rhys's dark red Jaguar coming up the drive. She felt a confusing rush of gladness as though, quite apart from needing a mainstay, she was pleased he was here.

'Mari, it's wonderful to see you,' Gerallt declared.

'You, too,' his sister exclaimed as he squeezed her warmly.

Her unhappiness temporarily forgotten, Meredith laughed. 'Hello, Uncle Dan!'

'How's my favourite niece?' he asked, hugging her.

'All the better for seeing you!'

The next few minutes were lost amid the general confusion of a family reunion. Everyone seemed to be talking at once as Rhys got out of his Jaguar and strolled with prowling masculine grace towards the group.

Meredith's gaze went to him, her lips curving in a smile.

'Hi,' he greeted her.

Mari broke off from her conversation with her brother as she noticed him.

'You must be Trefor!' she declared warmly. 'Meredith's mentioned you in her letters!'

'No, I'm Rhys, Rhys Treherne,' he smiled, offering his hand.

Meredith could see that already her aunt was taken with his charm. As the introductions were completed, Dan said in his friendly drawl,

'With a Christian name like Rhys you must be Welsh.'

'I'm more Cornish than Welsh, but my grandmother came from round here,' Rhys told him.

'All the best people come from round here,' Jessica put in, drawing laughter from the others.

'So what's become of the young doctor you were dating?' Mari asked Meredith.

She had been staring coldly at her sister-in-law and the question made her heart plummet. She hesitated, aware of everyone waiting for her to answer. She felt Rhys's hand at her back and she was very glad of its support.

'Actually, that...that's something I'm going to have to explain to everyone,' she said awkwardly. 'You see, in the paper tomorrow there's going to be an announcement...'

Her voice caught and faltered and, as it did, Rhys stated calmly, 'An announcement of our engagement. Meredith's agreed to marry me.'

'But I——' Her bewildered protest was cut off as his mouth swooped to silence her with his kiss.

Tender yet ardent, it was over before she had time almost to register the feel of his lips, or to recover from his false declaration. As he raised his head she stared into his eyes. The dark light she saw in them seemed to hold her spellbound, and her chance to speak out was lost as a babble of voices broke in on them.

CHAPTER NINE

IT WASN'T till later that Meredith had the chance to talk to Rhys alone. She returned from showing her aunt upstairs to find that her father was helping Dan carry the luggage in from the car. The events of the last half-hour had left her in a state of total confusion. She felt as if she were dreaming. In a while she would wake up, surely.

But Rhys looked real and solid enough as she entered the drawing-room. He was seated on the sofa chatting to Margred, who was collecting up the teacups.

'Where's Jessica?' she began as she saw that her sister-in-law had disappeared.

'Her headache's worse and she's gone to lie down,' Rhys told her. He stretched out his hand, his voice taking on a caressing warmth as he said, 'Come here.'

Margred smiled at them indulgently and went out discreetly with the tray. She seemed as pleased as Gerallt had been by the surprise announcement Rhys had sprung on everyone.

'Come here,' Rhys insisted softly.

Obeying him, Meredith asked in a bewildered voice, 'Rhys, what on earth's going on? Why did you say we're engaged?'

He took hold of her hand.

'It got you off the hook, didn't it?'

'But what about tomorrow?'

'You mean when *The Times* comes out,' Rhys guessed. 'Don't worry. The only announcement in it will be the correct one. I got on to the paper immediately after you left the mine. The way it will look to all and sundry is that you've fallen in love with me.'

The clasp that enfolded her fingers was firm and his eyes were a mesmerising blue. For an instant, as he spoke of her falling in love with him, she felt almost as if he was making a prediction. She shook off the quixotic notion.

'I still don't understand,' she faltered.

A glimmer of a smile softened the hard lines of Rhys's face.

'Good,' he said briefly.

'What do you mean, good?' she protested. 'You don't seem to realise what you've done!'

'Well, for one, I've saved your pride.'

That much was true. 'Yes . . . but . . .'

'But what?' he prompted as she trailed off.

She struggled to collect her thoughts. It wasn't easy when her mind was too dazed to function at all clearly.

'You've got me out of one awkward situation, only to land me in another!' she said.

'Why should you find it awkward being engaged to me?' he drawled, teasing her gently.

'But we're not engaged, not really.'

'What's not real about it?'

'You know as well as I do our engagement isn't genuine,' she said. 'I hardly expect you to marry me just to save my pride!'

'If you weren't happy with my solution why did you go along with it?' Rhys asked, watching her closely.

'Because...' she began and then found herself floundering. 'I...I was so astounded initially I...I didn't know what to say, and then by the time I'd recovered it was a *fait accompli*.' She didn't add that the furious glare Jessica had flashed her had also prompted her to keep quiet. It evened the score a little to know she was jealous. 'And...and then I suppose I was glad that you'd got me off the hook,' she concluded, using the same phrase he had used.

'I thought those were probably your reasons,' Rhys said, his voice a shade dry.

There was something in his inflexion that made her glance speculatively at him. But before she had a chance to reply Gerallt came into the room.

'Well, that's the luggage seen to,' he stated heartily. 'I'm sure Mari's brought ten times as much as she needs. She never did believe in travelling light.'

'You only think that because you never go away for longer than a couple of days,' Meredith told him. 'Aunt Mari's spending six weeks touring Europe and she'll need clothes for all sorts of weather.'

'Yes, I suppose so,' he smiled. 'Anyway that's not important. What is, is that you and Rhys are engaged. I'm delighted.'

'I'm glad you approve,' Rhys said. 'I should have asked your permission first, I know, but I got a bit carried away.'

'I like a man who knows his own mind,' Gerallt replied. Good humour twinkled in his eyes as he continued, 'Though if I hadn't given my permission I don't suppose it would have made any difference!'

Rhys laughed. 'I'm afraid it wouldn't,' he agreed.

As he spoke he glanced at Meredith, his gaze holding hers. She felt her heart give an odd little lurch. Their engagement was bogus yet when he looked at her that way, with a warmth she'd never seen before in the depths of his cobalt eyes...

For heaven's sake keep a grip on reality, something inside her warned. Rhys wasn't in love with her. He'd stepped in to help her, out of a sense of chivalry.

'How did Trefor take the news that you and Rhys are getting married?' her father asked her.

'He...' she faltered and then improvised as best she could, 'He... he was shocked at first...'

She was still jolted by his perfidy, and her voice caught a little.

'I'm sure you let him down lightly,' Gerallt said reassuringly. 'You know, I'd been worrying that Trefor wasn't right for you, but it seems it took Rhys to convince you of the fact.'

'You were worried?' she said, puzzled. 'You never breathed a word of it to me.'

'No, but I fully intended to talk to you about it,' Gerallt told her. 'I was afraid that perhaps you were thinking about marrying Trefor because you wanted to please me.'

'What?' Meredith asked blankly.

'Margred took me to task over it. She said I'd teased you about giving me some grandchildren for so long that you felt duty bound to do something about it,' her father told her.

'But that's ridiculous!' Meredith exclaimed, and then immediately searched her heart to see if there was a grain of truth in what the housekeeper had said.

'I'd guessed that Rhys was interested in you but it wasn't until the other evening I realised it was mutual,' Gerallt remarked.

Rhys slanted a questioning glance in Meredith's direction. 'Is that so?' he commented. His voice was lazy but his blue eyes were very sharp.

'Yes, she has some very romantic notions about your ancestry,' Gerallt informed him.

'Dad!' she pleaded, blushing. She didn't want Rhys to know that she had likened him to a Cornish wrecker.

'All right, all right, I won't say any more,' her father laughed.

They were joined by her aunt and uncle and a short while later Margred interrupted to say that dinner was ready. Gerallt sat at one end of the table with Meredith and Rhys facing Mari and Dan.

'How long have you known each other?' Mari smiled. She added cauliflower and carrots to the meat on her plate then passed the vegetable dish to her husband. 'Am I right in guessing it's been a whirlwind romance?'

'Whirlwind and stormy,' Rhys replied with humour.

His cobalt eyes seemed to tease as he smiled at
Meredith. She felt her pulse flutter nervously but
managed to smile back at him.

'Is there any chance of your engagement being
a whirlwind affair, too?' her aunt asked. 'I'd love
to be at your wedding, and we don't fly back to
the States until the very end of July.'

Alarmed by the way her sham engagement
seemed to be gaining a momentum of its own,
Meredith began, 'But we can't poss——'

A firm hand dropped over hers. Cutting in
before she inadvertently gave the game away,
Rhys promised, 'I'll see what I can do to talk
Meredith into being a summer bride.'

After her one near slip, Meredith let Rhys do
the talking. He seemed much more skilled at
handling the conversation than she was, and she
was glad when unobtrusively he steered it on to
another topic.

The meal came to an end and they had coffee
in the drawing-room. As she leaned forward to
set her cup down on the low onyx table, Rhys
laid his arm along the back of the sofa. She relaxed back to find herself virtually in his embrace.

Her head was in enough of a whirl without his
touching her, but before she could ease unobtrusively away his hand dropped on to her shoulder.
He'd made their engagement seem so convincing
that she was in danger of forgetting it was a piece
of play-acting!

He kept her in the circle of his arm until he
stood up to leave. Realising that it was expected
of her, she accompanied him into the hall. 'That
all seemed to go off very smoothly,' Rhys re-

marked when they were well out of earshot in the porch.

'It won't be so good when there's a broken engagement,' she answered wryly.

'That's a bridge we'll cross if and when we get to it,' he said.

Her gaze flew to his. 'If?' she questioned.

'You may decide you like being engaged to me,' he answered.

His tone was mocking, but there was something in the depths of his eyes that made her ask hesitatingly, 'Rhys, you don't seriously want to marry me, do you?'

A smile etched grooves in his tanned cheeks. 'It would be one way of getting you into my bed,' he answered.

She had been seeking honesty from him. Instead he gave her a wolfish quip that sent a sensual ripple over her skin and set a match to her temper.

'Well, you won't do it any other way, I can assure you!' she declared.

'I wouldn't count on it,' Rhys answered. 'After all,' he mocked, 'if you're not attracted to me, why are you standing there wondering if I'm going to kiss you goodnight?'

The fact that the thought had gone through her mind made a blush stain her cheeks. Knowing that it betrayed her, she began furiously, 'If I weren't indebted to you . . .'

'But you are,' Rhys reminded her. 'And since doubtless your family will expect us to take our time saying goodnight, we'd better do things properly.'

Before she realised his intention, he gathered her towards him, his mouth coming down on hers. She pushed at his shoulders in the brief instant before his kiss, hard, deliberate and possessive, sent a shock wave of pleasure through her.

She tried to fight the physical response but it was no use. She could feel him against her, his body, lean and hard, feel her nipples tightening as her breasts were crushed softly against his chest.

A faint moan escaped her as her lips parted under his. Her response was bewildered and yet passionate and, encouraging it, Rhys moved to hold her more intimately still. A knowing hand caressed the curve of her back as he explored her mouth with his own.

When the kiss finally ended, she opened her eyes slowly, more than a little dazed. There was a glitter of satisfaction in the cobalt gaze that met hers.

'You kiss me back very sweetly,' Rhys murmured huskily. 'Are you sure you're not just a little in love with me, without knowing it?'

'Yes...' she said, not at all sure of anything at that particular moment. She paused. 'But... but I think we need to talk, or this bogus engagement of ours could well get out of hand.'

'Tomorrow's Saturday, so why don't we spend the day together?' Rhys said. Something in his tone made her search his masculine features. The stern set of his jaw suggested displeasure. 'That should give us ample time to work out how we play things from here.'

'Rhys, you're not cross with me are you?' she asked hesitantly.

'Why would I be cross with you?' he asked.

'Well...for landing you in all this.'

A smile touched the corners of his mouth as he said, 'It's a bit of a tangle, but no doubt we'll sort it out in the end.'

He called for her at just after eleven the following morning, looking tanned and very fit in a blue and grey checked shirt and well-cut grey trousers. She heard Jessica's step on the stairs as she crossed the hall to answer the doorbell.

She was expecting Rhys, yet, even so, as she opened the front door her pulse fluttered a little, a reflex response to his raw masculinity.

'Hi,' he said. 'I see you're ready.'

As he spoke his cobalt eyes ran their appraising gaze over her. His look was flattering and sensual, and she caught her breath a little. Hoping he hadn't noticed her reaction to him, she adjusted the flipped-up collar of her white short-sleeved blouse. With it she wore a desert-beige skirt. A button-through opening on each side of the front panel accentuated the skirt's flattering line.

'I...I'll just get my jacket,' she told him. 'Come in for a minute.'

She led the way into the hall, aware of his footfall, lithe and as sure as a cat's, close behind her.

Her sister-in-law had paused at the foot of the stairs, one slim hand resting lightly on the newel-post. She looked graceful and poised as ever in a ballerina-style top and finely tapered trousers.

'Hello, Jessica,' Rhys greeted her. 'How are you feeling this morning?'

Jessica flicked her ash-blonde plait over her shoulder.

'Much better, thanks,' she smiled. 'And how are you feeling as a newly engaged man?' she teased.

Meredith observed their exchange, the line of her sensitive mouth tight. Was it any wonder that Trefor had been beguiled by her sister-in-law?

Slim, elegant and blonde, Jessica knew how to fascinate. She's got mystique and I haven't, Meredith thought turbulently, unaware that her sparkle and fire were every bit as potent as Jessica's cool languid sex-appeal. To erode her self-confidence still further, grooves appeared in Rhys's lean cheeks, confirming that he was aware of Jessica's charm.

'I think you know enough about men to guess how I'm feeling,' he drawled in reply.

At that moment the drawing-room door opened and Gerallt came into the hall.

'Ah, Rhys, I thought I heard your voice,' he said. 'You're just the person I wanted to see. Can you spare a minute? I want your personal opinion on an investment scheme. I've got the details in my study.'

'Dad, it is Saturday!' Meredith protested.

'Decisions have to be taken even at weekends,' Rhys reminded her. 'I won't be long.' He tossed the keys to his Jaguar to her. 'Do you want to wait in the car?'

'Perhaps I'll drive off without you,' she quipped, joking with him for her father's benefit.

Amused by her manufactured flash of mischief, Rhys returned, 'You do, my little elf, and I'll catch up with you later.'

The sensuality of his voice, coupled with the endearment, implied an intimacy between them which sent a little shiver tracing over her skin. He followed Gerallt into the study, leaving her alone with Jessica.

She wasn't sure she could bring herself to be civil to her sister-in-law now she knew the truth about her and Trefor. She headed towards the porch to avoid having to speak to her.

Jessica fell into step beside her. False as ever, she began as if they were the best of friends, 'You certainly took us all by surprise yesterday.'

'Yes, I suppose I did.' Meredith's brief answer, which was as much as she could manage, sounded casual.

They emerged from the porch where Jessica halted. 'I have to applaud your skill,' she said. Tilting her head to one side, she studied Meredith in the bright sunlight. 'You've played Rhys and Trefor off against each other very nicely. I'm not usually fooled by anyone, but you fooled me completely. I'd no idea it was Rhys you wanted to spur on. I thought it was Trefor. You must be feeling very pleased with yourself.'

Meredith clenched her hand tightly on the car keys in her palm. She, too, had been fooled! She had believed Jessica was her friend. Unable to say what she'd have liked to because that would

have given the game away, she replied, 'Do I
detect a note of envy, Jessica?'

Anger flickered for an instant in her sister-in-
law's blue eyes. But her voice was lazy and held
a note of mockery as she answered, 'Don't con-
gratulate yourself too soon. Engagements can be
broken.'

She turned and walked back inside the house,
while Meredith went to sit on the wall beside
Rhys's car. From a distance she looked as serene
as the garden statue that graced the rose garden.
Close to, her fascinating amber eyes were stormy.

She glanced up, hearing Rhys's firm tread on
the gravel. He came towards her with his masculine prowling stride.

'Let's go,' he said.

She stood up from the wall and brushed her
skirt. 'I'll drive?' she said, more than a hint of
challenge in her tone.

Rhys's gaze narrowed on her a little. 'You've
got the keys. Go ahead,' he agreed.

His easy acquiescence was not at all what she'd
hoped for.

'I thought you might be one of those men who
object to being driven by a woman,' she teased.
Jessica had been needling her, but in Rhys's
company she quickly forgot her irritation.

'I'm very liberal-minded,' Rhys said
mockingly.

She got into the Jaguar and adjusted the seat
which, to accommodate his long legs, was set too
far back for her.

'Where are we going?' she asked.

'To Betwys-y-Coed,' he said. 'I thought we'd admire the falls and then have lunch somewhere.'

'Sounds good,' she agreed.

Starting the engine, she pulled away, sending the gravel chips flying.

'I was surprised when you said yesterday that your grandmother came from round here,' she remarked. 'Is that why you're interested in local history?'

'Got it in one,' he answered.

The car handled beautifully and she drove competently, steering the Jaguar round the sharp curves with ease. Rhys sat beside her, the rush of wind from the open sun-roof ruffling his dark hair, his profile arrogantly carved.

Raising his voice above the noise of slip-stream, Rhys drawled, 'Do you feel like telling me now what this display of independence this morning is all about?'

'Don't you like being driven?' she asked.

'Stop stalling and tell me what was needling you earlier.'

She was impressed and just a little antagonised by his perceptiveness. 'You're always in control of every situation, aren't you?' she said.

'And you don't like that,' he guessed, amused by her remark.

She was tempted to agree with him out of sheer perversity. Yet the truth was his undertone of firmness appealed to her. It had done from the first though she'd refused to admit it.

They came to the Swallow Falls and she parked in the shade alongside several other cars and two coaches. Although the falls were a popular beauty spot, they met few people as they strolled along the forest path towards the sound of rushing water. Sunlight shafted through the trees, dappling the glade.

'It's even lovelier here than I remembered,' Meredith breathed.

'Look!' As he spoke the quiet command, Rhys took hold of her arm, drawing her attention to a grey squirrel that went leaping across the path.

Aware of them, it froze, and then, as they stayed still, it bounded towards a nearby oak, climbed the trunk and went running along a branch. Sharing the moment with Rhys, she realised suddenly that it was not the first moment of perfect understanding they had shared.

The sound of voices heralded people approaching and the squirrel promptly vanished. She exchanged a smile with Rhys, who slipped his arm around her waist. It remained there as they continued along the path to the falls.

They found a good vantage point and stood for some time watching the tumbling rushing water that streamed over the rocks. Sunlight sparkled on the ceaseless cascade, while white tongues of froth surged forward at the base of the falls to meet the plunging torrent. The crystal-clear water whirled and eddied, while overhead the oaks spread a dappled shade, the shafts of light filtering through the leaves to sparkle in a thousand sunbeams.

Later they took the path which followed the boulder-strewn course of the river. She enjoyed the walk downhill, but was glad to pause and catch her breath on the steep climb back.

Rhys skimmed a stone across the water and then joined her where she sat on a sloping outcrop of rock.

'This is a very peaceful spot,' he said as he drew her into his arms.

She leaned back against his chest. The sun was warm and the river chuckling over its stony bed added to the sense of tranquillity. Without meaning to, she let her fingers caress the strong hands that were linked about her waist.

'I don't know about you, but I'm getting hungry,' she murmured with a soft smile.

'Me too,' he said, a husky note to his voice.

As he spoke he swept her hair away from her neck, pressing his lips to her nape, while his hands slid down her lightly tanned arms.

She felt her senses stir at his touch. Her pulse began to beat faster and quickly, before the exciting tingling of her blood could grow any stronger, she said, 'Rhys, don't.'

'Why not?' he murmured. Gently and very sensuously he bit her earlobe. 'We're engaged, aren't we?'

She pushed at his hands, part of her wanting him to continue, part of her wishing that he would ignore her resistance.

'We're pretending to be engaged.'

'OK, then let's stop pretending,' he said, 'and I'll ask you properly this time. Will you marry me, Meredith?'

Her heart skipped a beat. She glanced up over her shoulder at him. 'Are you . . . making fun of me?' she stammered.

His jaw clenched a little with impatience. 'Do I sound as if I am?' he said.

'No... but...' She turned her head and let her gaze return to the river.

Her heart was thumping erratically; her thoughts raced. Why was the word yes on the tip of her tongue? Her pride wasn't so fragile, surely, that she needed to accept Rhys's proposal because of the look of things?

Before she could answer the question her mind had framed, Rhys stood up. Reaching for her hand, he drew her to her feet. His black hair gleamed in the sunlight.

'I see I've taken you by surprise,' he said.

'You have,' she agreed breathlessly. 'I...' She turned away, took a couple of agitated steps towards the river and then spun back to face him. 'I... I don't understand you at all.'

'What don't you understand?'

'Why you want to marry me.'

His masculine gaze slid over her slim figure and as it did so a faint blush came into her cheeks. It betrayed that she was every bit as aware of the potent sexual chemistry between them as he was.

'Is it really such a puzzle?' he said.

'You want me in bed.' The blunt words were out before she could stop them, prompted by an odd catch of disappointment. She would have liked that to be only one of the ways he wanted her, she realised.

'I don't generally find it necessary to propose marriage to get a woman into bed with me,' he mocked.

Remembering the evening of the party, she was sure of it. He had made her forget everything save the sweet magic of desire when he had kissed her. Sparks came into her amber eyes as she thought of the affairs he must have had.

The next instant they faded. As the implication of his words hit her she faltered, 'Then...you're proposing to me for some deeper reason than just bed?'

'There are a number of reasons why I'm suggesting we get married,' Rhys told her. 'One of them is that I want a son.'

'And...the other reasons?' she ventured, and then held her breath.

'We enjoy each other's company. We like the same things. You turn me on physically. In every way you're very stimulating to have around.'

'That's very complimentary,' she said, and didn't know why she felt let down suddenly and hurt.

'But it's not enough?' he guessed, his tone a shade clipped.

'If you were in love with me it might be...but...'

'Are you telling me that if I were in love with you you'd marry me?' Rhys prompted, cutting in.

Was that what she was telling him? It couldn't be. And yet it was. It had to be, because she heard herself say out loud, 'Yes.'

Something glittered in the depths of Rhys's eyes. 'In which case I have a confession to make,' he said softly, drawing her into his arms. 'I fell in love with you the very first time I met you.'

CHAPTER TEN

THEY had been engaged for two short weeks when she realised that she was in love with him, too, hopelessly in love, and had been for days, perhaps weeks, without knowing it. It was a hot Saturday afternoon and they had driven to a secluded cove.

Surrounded by tall cliffs, it was off the beaten track, but well worth the steep scramble down, for they had the small sandy beach completely to themselves. The incoming tide washed over the rocks near to the shore, while the sea, which stretched away to the blurred blue curve of the horizon, shimmered and danced in the sun.

Meredith crossed her arms, took hold of the hem of her white top and pulled it over her head to reveal the navy and white bikini she wore underneath. She shook her silky hair into place and then coloured with a flush of sexual awareness as her gaze inadvertently met Rhys's.

He ran his eyes down her, admiring her full firm breasts and the curve of her legs as she stood slender, tanned and bare-footed. She felt her pulse quicken and, needing to break the strange exciting tension between them, asked, a husky catch in her voice,

'Did...you swim a lot in South Africa?'

The smile he gave her seemed to stop her breathing for an instant. It was both knowing and attractive and she wondered if he knew what had prompted her question.

'The mines were well inland,' he told her, 'so I didn't get much of a chance. When I did have a few weeks' holiday I spent them on the coast. The beaches are wonderful.'

She sat down. Gazing seawards while he unfastened his jeans, she said, 'I expect they put this little cove in the shade.'

'No way,' came the answer. 'Don't ever be on the defensive for what you have here in North Wales. Just at this moment, for me, it's the next best place to paradise.'

'Really?' she said, glancing up.

Stripped, he was like some bronze statue except that no statue had dark curling hairs on thighs and chest. Virility and power were stamped into his physique. She saw that red swimming-trunks hugged his lean hips.

He sat down beside her and her gaze went skittishly to his wonderful chest and shoulder muscles. The next instant she gave a little gasp as he took hold of her. He leaned back on the sand, pulling her playfully down with him.

'Really,' he confirmed.

'Rhys, let go!' she laughed, pushing her hands against his chest.

He ignored her request. Keeping her his prisoner, he rolled over, trapping her beneath him. Gently he tucked a strand of her hair behind her ear.

'The beach is lovely in its own right, but it's even lovelier because we're here together, together and alone,' he said.

She could feel the hardness of his thighs against her own. The sand was warm against her back and his eyes were a mesmerising blue.

He bent his head and, as he did so, she wound her arms tightly about his neck. The kiss they exchanged was sweet and lingering.

'We're lucky,' she murmured when his lips left hers. 'Only a few people know about this cove.'

'Is this where Jessica comes to swim?' Rhys said, his thumb caressing her cheek.

Meredith turned her head to press a kiss into his palm. 'Yes. Why?'

'Just that I hope she isn't planning on coming here today,' Rhys answered, a wolfish glint in his eyes.

Her mouth tightened a little. Wanting to forget her treacherous sister-in-law, she murmured, 'So do I.'

Rhys gazed down at her, evaluating her reply. To her disappointment, instead of kissing her again, he released her.

'Have you and Jessica had some kind of dust-up?' he probed.

'What makes you say that?' she stalled. Refusing to let unpleasant memories spoil a beautiful afternoon, she joked, 'Because I'd rather she didn't join us?'

The grooves in Rhys's cheeks deepened. But though he was amused by her answer he didn't let the topic drop. 'No, not because of that. I was wondering why she's not staying with you any more,' he said.

'She wanted to move back into her own place,' Meredith answered. 'Her house has been empty a long time...and...' She hesitated, hovering suddenly on the brink of telling him the full story.

'And we all know how dangerous it is to leave property empty round here.' There was a teasing light in Rhys's eyes as he finished the sentence for her.

She knew the sparring exchange he was referring to and laughed as she remembered the tilt. 'I was trying to warn you off,' she told him.

Rhys smiled, and her pulse fluttered as a look of sexual telepathy flashed between them, a telepathy which had been there from the first.

'I know,' he said huskily. He dropped a light kiss on her lips. 'Come on, let's take a swim before the sight of you in that very attractive bikini gets too much for me.'

The soft sliding sand became firm and wet beneath her feet as they approached the white-edged wavelets that broke with a little rush on the shore. Together they splashed into the sea and as they did so Meredith let go of his hand.

Rhys went ahead of her with a racing dive. She saw his strong tanned shoulders cleaving through the water and, a good swimmer herself, she launched into a stylish crawl, following the course he had taken.

When at last she drew level with him he was some way out in the bay. The sea lapped his chest as he grinned at her. With his black hair slicked down and gleaming wet, his strong good-looking features were emphasised.

'Were you trying to race me?' he teased.

'I might have succeeded if you hadn't had a head start,' she said with bravado, and then gave a little squeal as he went to duck her for her cheek.

She swam away quickly to escape him. She knew he was gaining on her and turned to splash him as his arm encircled her waist. He pulled her close, the contact with his hard man's body sending a thrill through her.

'What was that you said?' he demanded, mock-threatening.

Mischief danced in her amber eyes. 'I said——' she began defiantly, and then was silenced by his mouth.

Her fingers tightened on his gleaming shoulders as they both submerged themselves together. The eroticism of his near-naked body and his lips which coaxed hers to part for him was heightened by the cool silent darkness all around them.

Down they went, wet legs entwining, until she broke free from him, needing air. She came to the surface, gasping. The sun dazzled overhead and the roar of the sea sounded once more. Rhys's dark head surfaced beside her. He shook the water from his face.

'You kiss even better than you swim,' he chuckled.

'You seem to excel at both!' Her voice was laughing and breathless.

Knowing that she couldn't hope to race him back, she launched into a graceful breast-stroke. She reached the shallows and then ran up the beach to flop down on the sand.

While she towelled herself dry, her gaze lingered on him. Having headed close to the shore with her, he had now turned to float on his back.

She gathered her hair in her fingers at her nape and twisted it over her shoulder, squeezing the moisture from it as she watched his strong but leisurely back crawl.

The sun was hot and she reached for her suntan cream. She had oiled herself earlier, but most of it had washed off with her swim.

'Let me do that for you,' Rhys said as he joined her.

A warm knowing hand smoothed the fragrant oil on to her skin. She surrendered to the pleasurable sensations his touch aroused and then clutched at her bikini top as he slid the straps over her arms. His palm moved over her shoulders.

'Do you want me to oil you now?' she asked as he finished, glad that her back was to him and that he couldn't see she was blushing.

'No, I'm darker-skinned than you are,' he said, reclining lazily. 'I tan easily.'

She looped her arms round one raised knee. For a while neither of them spoke. A contented tiredness was settling over her after her swim. She was aware of Rhys stretched out indolently on the warm sand beside her.

Presently she murmured, 'I haven't felt happy like this for ages.'

'How long?' Rhys wanted to know.

She thought for a moment. Her brother's car crash, she realised, had been like a watershed in her life. Until then, although she'd been seeing a lot of Trefor, she hadn't been serious about him.

'Not since Stephen was alive,' she said. 'I haven't felt happy or carefree like this since then.' She turned her head to glance at Rhys. He was lying with his eyes closed, his lashes dark against the carved line of his cheeks. 'It makes me think you must be good for me,' she said, teasing charm in the lilt of her voice.

A smile touched his very masculine mouth. His eyes remained closed. 'Have you only just discovered that?' he mocked. He sounded sleepy and content.

She relaxed back on the sand, listening to the call of the sea and the cry of the gulls. She and Rhys didn't touch, not even their hands. The silence lengthened between them, an undemanding silence in which she felt closer to him than she had ever felt to anyone before. It was as if they were both at one with the sea, the sky and the surrounding mountains.

She must have drifted off, because for an instant when her lashes fluttered up she couldn't think where she was. A long pleasant dream hovered on the edge of her memory. It was somehow connected with Rhys and, trying to recall it, she rolled on to her front.

He appeared to be asleep and, taking advantage of the opportunity it gave her, she let herself study the strong lines of his face. His thick hair fell in dark disarray across his brow. Beneath it were the carved Italianesque features; black hawkish eyebrows, straight nose and a mouth that was firm, good-tempered and as masculine as the rest of him. She noted the cleft in his chin that gave his face character, amazed at the pleasure it gave her to gaze at him.

I love him, she thought, dazed. She had never known until now what an all-consuming passion love was. To add to the sense of wonder which filled her, she realised suddenly that her affection for Trefor had only ever been a mere shadow compared with the strength of her feelings for Rhys.

When had she first fallen in love with him? From the beginning? It wasn't possible. And yet... And yet why else had she been so haughty and defensive with him, so willing always to oblige him with an argument, so feverish and dizzy when he kissed her...?

Her heart full of wonderment, she brushed the exciting line of his jaw with her fingertips and whispered, 'Oh, Rhys...'

Immediately his eyes opened, locking with hers. Electricity flickered along her nerves.

'I thought you were asleep,' she breathed.

His hand slipped beneath the silken fall of her hair. 'You intoxicate me,' he murmured, his voice low, husky and compelling.

Her pulse fluttered as her gaze slipped to his mouth. Obeying a sweet impulse, she bent her head. Her lips were soft as they moved across his, exploring the shape of his mouth. Rhys's arms tightened around her waist, pressing her body to his as he took over the kiss she had initiated.

Pleasure licked along her veins. He kissed her tenderly, but with a consuming passion that made her ache for more. He rolled over, trapping her beneath him. She could feel the hardness of his frame against the slightness of her form, and she slid her hands over his bronzed shoulders, her fingers delighting in the warm smooth texture of his skin.

Her moan of protest when at last his mouth left hers changed to a sigh of pleasure as his lips traced the line of her cheekbone. Gently, knowingly, he found each sensitive place, touching and kissing her until need for him was a hunger that heated her blood.

She ran her fingers through his hair and then, as he drew back from her, whispered, scarcely knowing what she was saying, 'Rhys, don't stop. Please don't stop.'

'You don't have to ask,' he muttered raggedly. 'I want you, Meredith. From the first moment I met you I've wanted you.'

He found her mouth again, while his hand travelled up her slim back, dealing deftly with the clasp of her bikini top. Cupping her breast, he put his mouth to it, his hard lips becoming gentle as they closed over her nipple.

An agonising shaft of pleasure pierced her and she dug her fingers into his shoulders, wanting his assault on her senses never to end. It was as if he meant to kiss, caress, and taste every inch of her. She pressed her lips against the strong column of his throat. Made bold by her need, her hands caressed his hot skin, thrilling to the muscles beneath her palms.

At the back of her mind was the knowledge that, unless she stopped responding to him, their mutual desire could have only one conclusion.

Loving him, glorying in his caresses, the demands of his mouth on hers, it was what she wanted.

His breath was warm on her skin as he bent to slide her bikini briefs away from her slim thighs. The sun was bright overhead and the sea still called but, naked beneath him, she was no longer aware of either.

The delight Rhys took in her had her senses rushing. The swell of her breasts, the hollow at the base of her throat, her slender waist, the curve of her hips, all knew the touch of his lips and hands. It set her aflame, this hungry adoration of her body by the dominant man she had fallen so deeply in love with. Rhys's caresses grew ever more intimate, and she cried out as the ecstasy gathered to a pitch so intense she felt she couldn't bear it.

She moaned his name and, as she did so, he entered her, his strong frame covering hers. Her fingers tightened on his back with the slight pain of his first penetration and then dug into his flesh as pleasure overpowered her. Small cries escaped her, each thrust bringing her closer to the shattering moment of release.

And then, suddenly, came a star-burst of sensation that seemed to explode throughout her whole body. Rhys groaned, a long shudder of consumation racking him as her teeth cut into his shoulder.

Afterwards, the ripples of response fading slowly, she lay limp and warm beneath him, aware of the hammer strokes of his heart that matched hers beat for beat. For what seemed a pleasure-drugged eternity neither of them moved.

Then Rhys rolled on to his back, gathering her tenderly in his arms so that she lay with her head against his chest. She listened to the restless call of the waves, the cry of the gulls overhead as they circled the white cliffs.

Everything was the same as it had been earlier, except that now she was his woman. She belonged to him, body and soul, the radiance that enveloped her a part of the joy of oneness with him.

Beneath her cheek his deep chest rose and fell in a sigh of satisfaction. His palm stroked the gentle curve of her spine, his afterplay as tender as his lovemaking had been passionate.

'I always knew you'd be incredible,' he murmured.

She lifted her head to meet his gaze.

'And deep down I think I always knew that some day you'd seduce me,' she whispered. She touched his lips lightly with the tip of her forefinger, remembering his urgency, and his control. 'You were very careful not to hurt me.'

'It was your first time. I wanted you to love every minute of it,' he told her. Kissing her lightly on the lips he said, 'But, beautiful as it was just now, I don't intend making love to you in snatched moments on the beach. It's time we set a date so I can enjoy you in my arms, in my bed every night.'

The bubble of joy inside her made her tease, 'Why all the rush?'

'I'm crazy about you,' he growled, pinning her down on the sand beneath him.

'I'm crazy about you, too,' she admitted, winding her hands happily about his neck as she met the downward movement of his mouth.

It was some while later when they left the beach. They returned to his house. Closing the front door behind them, Rhys drew her into his arms. 'You taste of sun and sea,' he murmured.

'And sand,' she whispered, a husky laugh in her throat. 'I can feel it between my toes.'

'You won't after we've showered together.'

'Together . . .?' After the way they'd made love on the beach it was ridiculous to blush, and yet that was exactly what she was doing.

Amusement at her reaction tempered the glitter of desire in his eyes.

'There's no point wasting hot water,' he teased.

They washed off the saltiness of the sea under the shower, exchanging kisses and caresses beneath the warm pelting water, and then they made love again in the large double bed.

Later Rhys put some steak under the grill while she prepared a salad. A sparkling wine accompanied the meal and, wrapped up in each other, the evening flew.

'Leave that,' Rhys said as she stood up to clear the table. Taking her by the hand, he led her over to the sofa, where he pulled her on to his lap. 'It's time I took you home,' he said.

'Dad knows I'm with you. He won't be worried about me.'

'I know,' Rhys answered, nibbling her ear, 'but I thought I'd come in with you and tell your family we've decided on a July wedding.'

Mari and Dan were chatting with her father in the drawing-room very much as she had expected they would be when she and Rhys walked in. The surprise was that her sister-in-law had called round for the evening.

'How nice to see you, Meredith,' Jessica greeted her, her eyes cool and taunting.

Meredith rallied quickly. 'You, too,' she lied for the sake of politeness.

'What will you have to drink, Rhys?' Gerallt asked.

'I can certainly recommend your father's malt,' Dan told him, raising the glass of whisky he was cradling.

'A drop of malt would round the evening off nicely,' Rhys said. He glanced at Meredith, 'Especially as I'm in the mood to celebrate.'

Mari was delighted with their news. 'July's a lovely month for a wedding,' she declared with a pleased smile. 'And Dan and I will be back from Europe by then.'

Jessica turned the languid charm of her eyes on Rhys. 'Evidently you don't believe in long engagements,' she said.

'You're right, I don't,' he agreed mockingly.

Meredith wondered why her sister-in-law had dropped in. She had no desire to entertain her. But Jessica, completely at home on the sofa, seemed to have settled down for the remainder of the evening. It was Rhys who was the first to leave.

Meredith saw him out and they kissed in the romantic shadows of the porch.

'I'll see you tomorrow,' Rhys murmured throatily at last.

'I love you,' she whispered against his cheek.

He took her face between his hands, his eyes holding hers captive. Then his lips came down on hers again, his hands warm on her back as his mouth explored hers with a deep tender passion.

She emerged from his embrace, her pulses throbbing. They said goodnight and she gazed after him as he strode towards his car. He returned her smile and then ducked into the driving seat.

She closed the front door and leaned against it dreamily for a moment before returning to the hall. A prettily curved gilt mirror graced the wall and, as she walked past it, she glimpsed her reflection. She paused, startled by the misty glow in her eyes. A new softness, a kind of inner beauty, showed in her face.

'You've fallen for him hard, haven't you?'

Meredith pivoted to see her sister-in-law. She was standing poised and derisive with the closed door to the drawing-room behind her.

'When women fall in love, however foolishly, they always look radiant,' she observed.

'I'm not foolish falling in love with Rhys,' Meredith answered. 'We're made for each other.'

The blue eyes that regarded her held a spiteful glitter.

'You think so? I wonder if you'll still think so when you've seen this.' Opening her clutch-bag,

Jessica took out an envelope. She handed it to Meredith.

'What is this?' Meredith asked.

'A little engagement present for you,' Jessica mocked.

Not sure what cat-and-mouse game her sister-in-law was playing, but wanting to put an end to it, Meredith tore open the envelope. Inside was a newspaper cutting.

'It's from the local paper where Rhys comes from,' Jessica told her.

Making no comment Meredith scanned the short article which was about the historical mining links between Cornwall and North Wales and then read with closer attention the final paragraph which concerned Rhys. It stated that as the new compounds technical director of the Mynydd-y-Glyn mine he was continuing in his grandfather's footsteps.

She glanced up. Her shoulders hunching in a little shrug, she said, 'I don't see the significance of this, I'm afraid. Am I supposed to be startled that Rhys's grandfather worked at the Mynydd-y-Glyn mine?'

'He did rather more than just work at the mine,' Jessica mocked. 'He owned it.'

Meredith knew that her surprise must be visible.

'Are you saying——?'

'Well done,' Jessica cut in ironically. 'I thought I might have to spell it out to you. Rhys is Tudor Morgan's grandson.'

'I...I don't believe you,' Meredith said, a thread of incredulity in her voice. 'Rhys would have told me.'

'You're the last person he'd have told. I wouldn't have found out either if I hadn't been rather clever,' Jessica said.

Meredith paced towards the large refectory table. If it was true what Jessica was saying, then why had Rhys never said anything to her? Brushing the question aside, she turned and demanded, 'So what if Rhys is Tudor Morgan's grandson?'

Jessica's lips curved in a contemptuous smile. 'Are you so in love with him you don't care that he's marrying you simply to regain his lost inheritance?' she asked.

'That's not true!' Meredith flashed.

'You mean you don't want it to be.'

'I mean you're lying!' Meredith told her. 'I love Rhys and I won't believe one word against him!'

Jessica looked at her scornfully. 'Ask yourself this,' she said. 'Why do you suppose Rhys came here when he'd worked in much larger mines in Canada and South Africa? Why do you think he chased you, proposed to you when you've scarcely known each other for more than——'

'Because he loves me!' Meredith cut in, her eyes full of sparks.

'I can understand your wanting to believe that.' Jessica tucked her clutch-bag under her arm. 'But don't think I haven't done my homework. Everything I've said, I can prove. I'm sure Rhys has told you he wants a son?'

Meredith's heart jolted. 'What of it?' she asked, her voice a shade tight.

Rhys meant everything to her. She couldn't bear it if his love was a sham.

'Just that if I were you I wouldn't give him one too soon,' Jessica replied. 'You see, once he's married you and has a son to inherit the mine when your father dies, he'll have won back what was taken from him. He won't need you any more. And as he's attracted to me . . .' She let her sentence hang in the air as she walked to the front door.

Meredith clutched at the table. So many thoughts were racing through her mind she felt almost dizzy. It was an effort to rally, but somehow she did.

'You're jealous!' she said with a flash of fire.

Jessica turned. 'Why don't you ask Rhys about it?' she suggested calmly as she went out into the night.

CHAPTER ELEVEN

MEREDITH slipped out of bed and paced over to the window. In a pale cream silk nightgown and with her flaming hair loose about her shoulders she looked like a pale ghost. Leaning against the sill, she gazed out at the morning, her eyes prickling.

She didn't want to believe a word Jessica had said to her the previous evening. She wouldn't believe a word of it! Of course Rhys loved her.

Yet why hadn't he told her about his background? Unable to answer the question, she dropped her head in her hands, doubts tearing her apart.

She'd spent the whole night trying to refute what her sister-in-law had told her. But all the time she kept remembering things, little things that were insignificant in themselves, but which added up, fostering a terrible uncertainty.

The playback of memory meant that she could vividly see Rhys, standing in the churchyard, reading the inscription on Tudor Morgan's tombstone. Was it local history he was interested in, or the grandfather who had disinherited him?

Then there was Glan-wern. Out of all the property on the market, why had he chosen to buy that particular house? It was large and rambling and the structural repairs he was having

173

done were running him up a colossal bill, he had said so himself.

He'd seemed surprised when she'd told him the house had once belonged to Tudor, but how could she be sure he hadn't known it all along? How could she be sure he hadn't bought Glanwern with the intention of reclaiming what should have been his by right?

A tear dropped into her palm. As it ran down her wrist she raised her head, swallowing hard against the tightness in her throat. She felt vulnerable, desperate, lost. If Rhys didn't love her, what was she to do?

Ask him, a reasonable voice insisted. Show him the newspaper cutting. I can't, came the agonised answer. I can't, because I'm afraid, because Jessica sounded so sure of herself when she suggested I confront him.

Wretchedly she stared out at the view of fields and mountains. Faint wisps of cloud drifted in a sky that was already turning a brilliant blue. The quietness of the summer morning seemed to mock the tumult of pain and uncertainty inside her.

Stop it, she told herself fiercely. Rhys loves you. You know he does. She thought of the deep, needful kisses they exchanged, the smoulder of passion in Rhys's dark eyes when he took her in his arms, the beauty and urgency of his lovemaking yesterday on the beach.

Why was she thinking the worst of him? He wasn't devious like Trefor. Immediately she wished she hadn't made the comparison. She'd been deceived by Trefor. Supposing Rhys was deceiving her too? Supposing he'd asked her to marry him solely because of the mine?

A chill smote her heart as she realised suddenly that, while she kept trying to convince herself he loved her, she'd only heard him say it once. It had been that day at the Swallow Falls, the day he'd proposed to her. From out of memory his voice spoke. 'Are you telling me that if I were in love with you you'd marry me?'

Unconsciously it was what she'd been telling him, but until that moment love hadn't entered the conversation. Instead Rhys had talked about wanting her physically, about wanting a son!

There was a telephone by her bedside. She snatched up the receiver, her hand trembling with the dread of her suspicions. The phone rang briefly and then his masculine voice, attractive and throaty, sounded in her ear. A lump came into her throat. Even had she known what she wanted to say she couldn't have spoken. As impulsively as she had picked up the receiver she put it down.

She brushed fingers across her forehead as she tried to think rationally, but how could she be rational when her love for Rhys was the core of her whole life? If what Jessica had told her was true, if she had to break off her engagement... The thought was like a knife-thrust straight into her heart.

It prompted her to action. She decided she must see Rhys before the uncertainty drove her crazy. She opened the door to her wardrobe. A jade skirt was the first garment that came to hand. She drew it out and slipped it on, teaming it with a striped cotton top.

Quickly she made up, emphasising her eyes with dusky shadow and mascara. A hint of blusher lent colour to her cheekbones. The lipstick she chose was a pretty shade of coffee-caramel.

It steadied her nerves a little to see that, despite the turmoil inside her, she looked composed and in charge of herself. Before her resolve could falter, she collected the newspaper cutting Jessica had given her and left her bedroom. Confronting Rhys was not going to be easy; she was so afraid of what she might learn.

Her car keys were on the table in the hall. She picked them up and went outside to her Peugeot, which was parked by the porch. She tossed her shoulder-bag on to the passenger seat beside her and pulled away down the drive.

Scarcely another car passed her in the quietness of the Sunday morning and she was soon at Glan-wern. She drew up in front of Rhys's Jaguar and got out. Her footsteps crunched on the gravel as she went to ring the bell.

Butterflies were fluttering in her stomach. Suddenly she wished fervently she hadn't come. It was ridiculously early. Rhys would still be in bed.

The next instant her agitated thoughts were cut short as he answered the bell. To her surprise, far from being half asleep he was shaved and ruggedly attractive in jeans and a white shirt. Her heart skipped a beat in response to his masculinity, the opening sentence she had rehearsed so carefully vanishing from her mind.

His shirt was undone at the throat, revealing the strong cords of his neck. She saw that his dark hair was wet from his shower, the gleaming strands unruly in a sensual sort of way.

Just to look at him was to be reminded of how much she loved him. If he didn't care for her in return, if his love was a lie, there would be nothing left in her life except the awful agony of heartbreak.

'Meredith!' he exclaimed. The chiselled lines of his face relaxed in a wide welcoming smile. 'You were the last caller I expected at this early hour. Come on in, sweetheart.'

She stepped over the threshold, nervousness making her babble, 'I was afraid you might not be up yet. As you say, it is early, but I couldn't sleep and ...'

She broke off as he closed the door behind her and drew her gently into his arms.

'I'm pleased to see you,' he murmured.

For a timeless moment she gazed back at him, the dark clamour of suspicion momentarily silenced as her senses swirled. Her hands stole up around his neck as he bent to her lips, a familiar pleasure licking along her veins. The kiss of greeting they exchanged was long, intimate and satisfying.

'Come through into the kitchen and we'll have breakfast together,' Rhys told her when finally he allowed her to breathe again. 'I've just made coffee and toast.'

She preceded him into the large sunlit kitchen, the tingling in her blood subsiding as she established a distance between them. The completeness of her response to him when he kissed her filled her with a sense of panic without her understanding why.

'Do you always get up so early on a Sunday?' she asked.

Her words sounded remarkably natural. They gave her time to catch her whirling thoughts.

'No, not usually,' he said with dry humour.

'Then what's special about today?' she asked.

'Some clown phoned me at just after six. Whoever it was rang off the moment I answered. As I was awake I decided to get up.'

'Oh,' she murmured with an awkward smile.

He set another place at the breakfast table and poured out the coffee. She watched him, aware of the animal grace of his movements, the snug fit of his jeans, the breadth of his shoulders.

'Would you like something cooked?' he asked.

'No, toast is fine,' she answered, taking her place at the table.

'Well,' Rhys prompted as he sat down opposite her, 'am I going to have to probe, or are you going to tell me what's behind this impromptu call?'

She still didn't know quite how she was going to begin and, stalling, she teased, 'I thought I was welcome any time.'

'You are,' he drawled. 'In fact I'm very flattered that after my kissing you goodnight the first thing you want on waking is for me to kiss you good morning.'

His smile was so attractive that it seemed almost to stop her breathing for an instant. She found herself smiling back and in that instant knew why a few minutes ago she had felt so panic-stricken.

She was so very much in love with him that if he lied to her she would believe him. She would want to believe him, want not to see, not to understand, not to admit that what Jessica was saying was the truth.

What point was there in confronting him outright when she would accept a lie from him blindly? Slowly she buttered her toast. So many emotions were warring inside her that she felt almost dizzy.

If only there was some way to test him, some way to find out the truth without his knowing it, so that he couldn't lie to her. And then, suddenly, it occurred to her that there was.

She reached for her shoulder-bag which was beside her chair, took out the newspaper cutting, and passed it to him. Despising herself for the deception, and yet able to think of no other way, she asked conversationally, 'Have you seen this?'

Rhys glanced at the cutting and then looked across at her, his dark brows drawn together quizzically. 'Where did you get this?' he enquired.

She brushed an imaginary crumb from her lap. 'It was in the local paper,' she lied. 'I...I thought you might be interested in it.'

His gaze returned to the cutting.

'Nice of them to give me a mention,' he commented as he set it aside.

'I didn't know your grandfather worked at the Mynydd-y-Glyn.' She spoke casually while unconsciously she clenched her fingers in suspense.

'Didn't you?' he said pleasantly.

'I'd like to know more about him.'

Rhys leaned back in his chair. 'Why this sudden interest in my grandfather?' he asked.

'You've never spoken about him. And I thought what a coincidence it was, his working at the mine...'

'And my not mentioning it,' he finished the sentence for her in the same tone as before, but she saw that his eyes held a glitter. It prepared her for the sudden slap of his napkin on the table. 'Just what is this?' he demanded. 'An inquisition?'

'No!' she protested. Her heart was thumping. Why was he angry if he had nothing to hide? 'I was just curious. If I'm going to marry you I need to know more about you.'

'If you're marrying me?' He was quick to pick her up on her choice of words. His jaw set grimly, he demanded, 'What the hell are you playing at, Meredith?'

'I'm not playing at anything.' She got to her feet so quickly that her undrunk coffee splashed into the saucer. 'And there's no need to lose your temper!'

He stood up from his chair. Biting out the words, he said, 'You're damned right I'm starting to lose my temper.'

'Because you can see your chance of owning the mine slipping away from you.' The accusation was out before she could help herself.

Something flickered across the rugged planes of his face. 'What did you say?' he demanded, his voice ominously calm.

She drew a quick steadying breath. This wasn't at all the way she'd meant to play it. But it was too late now for her to sound him out without his guessing. Her heart thumping, she said in a helpless rush, 'Rhys, I want to know if you're Tudor Morgan's grandson. I want to know if you really love me, or if you're marrying me to get control of the mine.'

'Did I hear that right?' he said. His voice vibrated with suppressed anger as he grabbed hold of her wrist.

'Is it true?' she sobbed.

'What do you think I am?' Rhys exploded. 'A liar, a schemer who needs to marry to get my hands on money? I could buy your father out tomorrow!'

Her gaze flew to his face, which was dark with rage. His reaction told her more convincingly than words that she'd accused him falsely. She was too relieved to be alarmed by the fire she saw smouldering in his eyes. What did it matter how furious he was with her as long as he loved her?

'Then you're not——' she faltered.

'No, I'm not Tudor Morgan's grandson,' he cut in as he released her wrist.

'Oh, Rhys, I . . . I'm sorry,' she whispered.

She was close to tears of relief. If only he would take her in his arms, forgive her for suspecting him, everything would be all right between them.

But he didn't look forgiving. He looked grim and perilous. It was the first time she'd seen him really angry. In a desperate attempt to make amends she said, 'Please don't be angry with me. I'm so ashamed for having doubted you.'

'That's nice to know,' he said sarcastically, 'especially when you had no evidence whatsoever for doubting me.'

He didn't spare the contempt in his voice, a contempt she knew she deserved. She didn't try to defend herself, only to explain.

'I was wrong,' she began, 'but when I read the newspaper cutting——'

'You jumped to the conclusion that Tudor Morgan must have had a grandson, that the grandson was me, and that I'd proposed to you because I wanted to get control of the Mynydd-y-Glyn.'

His stinging ridicule prompted her to flare in return, 'Why are you being so unforgiving? I've said I'm sorry. I wasn't to know what the cutting meant when it said you were following in your grandfather's footsteps by working at the Mynydd-y-Glyn.'

Rhys's voice was clipped. 'It refers to the fact that my grandfather, like me, was a mining engineer. He came here from Cornwall to build the engine house at the mine.'

'You mean the old engine house that's still standing? The one you mentioned when you borrowed the photograph album?' She was both surprised and interested by the revelation.

'Would you like proof of that as you're so sceptical about me?' Rhys asked sarcastically.

'No, of course not!'

Unappeased by her answer, Rhys scowled at her. 'Who put this whole idea into your head?' he demanded. 'Was it Trefor?'

'No!' she denied. She took a step towards him in appeal. 'Rhys, please...I know you're angry——'

'Smart of you.' The snap in his voice made her quickly withdraw the hand she'd been about to lay on his forearm. 'You didn't dream up anything as ridiculous as my being Tudor Morgan's grandson on your own. I suppose Trefor's still scheming to get you back.'

Suddenly she was angry too. Never noted for her cool reasoning when her blood was up, she said, 'Since you're not going to forgive me, why should you care whether he still wants me or not?'

The line of Rhys's mouth thinned. 'If you want to go back to him, feel free,' he told her.

If he had struck her in the region of her heart the shock and pain couldn't have been greater. She could feel the blood going from her face. It was over between them. He'd made it clear that it was.

She turned quickly and clutched at the edge of the worktop to steady herself. A sob rose in her throat. She strangled it before more than an anguished catch of breath could escape her. He heard it.

'Meredith?'

Her head jerked up as he came towards her. Pity from him would kill her! Pivoting, she said, 'A good thing I found out now, before we made the mistake of getting married.'

He frowned at her incoherent words. 'Found out what?' he questioned.

'That you don't care whether I walk away from you or not,' she choked.

Snatching up her shoulder-bag, she swept into the hall. She was at the front door so fast that Rhys had no chance to stop her.

'And it wasn't Trefor who told me you were marrying me for the mine,' she cried. 'It was Jessica!'

'Meredith, wait!'

His growled command checked her stride, but only for an instant. Then she was running towards her car.

She ducked into the driving seat, brushed her hand across her cheek to dry a tear, and started the ignition. In the mirror she glimpsed Rhys striding towards her. It added to her sense of panic, hurt and fury.

If she'd glanced at his face she would have seen that his anger had changed to masculine exasperation. But she didn't see. She engaged into what she thought was first gear, put her foot down hard on the accelerator and then gave a startled cry as the car shot backwards.

She slammed the brakes on too late to stop her Peugeot ramming into Rhys's Jaguar. In the instant's silence that followed the crash, she heard the tinkle of glass from his shattered headlamps.

Before she had a chance to recover, her door was opened. Seizing hold of her arm, Rhys hauled her out of the car. The ground felt unsteady under her feet.

He had been furious with her before. Now he would be livid.

'Rhys...I...' she stammered.

'I think this is where we came in,' he cut in drily. 'Are you OK?'

His words sounded far away. There couldn't be a note of wry amusement in his voice, not when she'd just smashed his headlamps. His features were blurred and, as the sickening fog thickened, she whispered, 'No...I...'

She remembered nothing more until she came round a few minutes later to find she was lying on the sofa in his lounge. She felt frighteningly weak and was reassured to see Rhys as her lashes fluttered up.

'Did I faint?' she murmured.

He nodded, his gaze, which was strangely tender, intent on her face. His hand grazed her cheek as he touched a strand of her hair. 'You went as pale as death and then keeled over,' he said. 'How are you feeling now?'

Her strength was returning already. The recollection of what had happened was slower to follow.

'I'm fine. Just a bit shaky, that's all.'

Rhys pushed her back against the cushions as she tried to sit up. 'Lie still for a while,' he told her.

Tall, lithe, and with a panther's grace in his tread, he went over to the drinks cabinet. She turned her head to watch him. As she did so, suddenly, the recollection came rushing back, the damage she'd done to his car, the row that had gone before.

'If you're getting me a drink,' she announced, 'I don't want one. I feel much better.'

The warring note in her voice made him turn. A dark eyebrow lowered at her and, seeing his expression, she decided she'd be wise to amend her tone.

'That sounds more like you,' he said. 'Well, if you've recovered, I've quite a few things I want to say to you.'

She could imagine!

'I...I'm sorry about your car,' she said. The pain of knowing it was she who had put an end to their relationship with her doubts was almost more than she could bear. She tried to hide it with defiance. 'But I'll pay for the damage as I did the last time.'

'Here, take a sip of brandy.' He offered her the glass.

She was always fierce when she was vulnerable, hurt, and his impersonal concern made her flare, 'I've told you I don't want it!'

He put the glass aside. 'I don't think there can be much wrong with you,' he said. 'There's certainly nothing wrong with your temper.'

'What do you expect——?' she began, and then gave a little frightened gasp as he took hold of her by the shoulders.

In a tone he had never used with her before, he said, 'Now you listen to me. I don't care how angry or upset you are, but that's the first and last time you storm out of here and leap into a car. Understood?'

She nodded. Swallowing hard, she said, 'I'm sorry about the damage.'

'Damn it, woman!' he said savagely, 'haven't you realised it yet? I'm not angry about my bloody car. I'm angry because you could have been hurt. Let me explain to you in words of one syllable, so that maybe you'll grasp what I'm trying to say. If, after we're married, you pull another stunt like the one you pulled just now, I'll put you across my knee and spank you.'

Her eyes flew to his. Her heart was suddenly beating so fast with hope and with relief that she couldn't speak.

'You mean...' she faltered. 'You mean you do still want me? I thought——'

'You shouldn't think,' he interrupted. 'You're not good at it.'

There was humour and tenderness in his blue eyes and suddenly she understood that his gentle mockery was all part of his loving her.

'Oh, Rhys...' she murmured in a choked voice.

Her arms went round him tightly as he pulled her against him. He took her chin between his thumb and forefinger, tilting up her face so that her lips could receive his kiss.

His mouth was tender and demanding and her own opened under it. Everything that was in her heart was mirrored in the sweetness with which she responded. She knew he was telling her that he loved her, knew it from the way he kissed her, the way he held her, and when finally he raised his head she saw it in his eyes.

An answering glow in her own, she whispered, 'I'm so sorry I doubted you, Rhys.'

The masculine line of his mouth quirked. 'Will you stop apologising to me?' he said.

'I'm sor...' she began contritely, and then laughed as she realised she was doing it again. 'You were so mad with me earlier, I can't seem to stop!'

Rhys chuckled. 'Now you know how I react when I'm jealous,' he said. 'I thought Trefor had spun you a crazy yarn to get you back, and, because deep down you were in love with him still, you'd fallen for it.'

'It was Jessica who spun me the yarn. I shouldn't have believed her, but there was such a horrible parallel between...'

'Between what?' Rhys prompted.

Her fingers smoothed the collar of his shirt, the movement unconscious and loving. 'She hinted that I was wrong about Trefor. I found out from him that they'd had an affair, the two of them. Because she hadn't been lying then I thought...'

'She wasn't lying about me, either,' Rhys guessed the rest of her sentence. 'Your sister-in-law seems to have a penchant for competing with you,' he concluded drily.

'What do you mean? Are you saying she offered herself to you?' Jealousy sharpening her perception, Meredith tumbled immediately to his oblique remark.

'She called round here with a report one evening and made it very plain that she was available,' Rhys told her. 'You'd told me Trefor had proposed and I was half out of my mind wondering how I was going to win you when you seemed hell-bent on marrying the toad. I was in no mood to flirt with Jessica.' An astute flicker crossed the chiselled planes of his face. 'So that's where the cutting she gave you came from!' he murmured, voicing the thought aloud as it occurred to him.

'Where?' Meredith asked.

His hands slipped beneath her top, stroking her warm skin.

'Forget your sister-in-law. Someone once said the best thing about a lovers' quarrel is making up. I intend to make up really well,' he growled. He started to nuzzle her neck.

A familiar melting pleasure ran along her veins. She was longing to be loved by him, to feel the warmth of his hands, the strength of his desire, but, knowing he was a man to understand playfulness as well as passion, she said, 'Stop a minute, Sherlock, and tell me.'

Amusement tempered the desire in Rhys's cobalt eyes.

'My stepfather sent me a copy of the local paper he takes. I recognised the article the moment you showed it to me. I'd left it somewhere about the room. When I turned Jessica down she must have slipped it into the papers she had with her, deciding she was going to make trouble for me in some way.'

'I played into her hands, didn't I?' Meredith said flirtatiously.

'And now you can play into mine,' Rhys quipped, as he ran his fingers erotically down her spine.

Accept 4 Free Romances and 2 Free gifts

•FROM READER SERVICE•

An irresistible invitation from Mills & Boon Reader Service. Please accept our offer of 4 free Romances, a CUDDLY TEDDY and a special MYSTERY GIFT... Then, if you choose, go on to enjoy 6 captivating Romances every month for just £1.60 each, postage and packing free. Plus our FREE newsletter with author news, competitions and much more.

Send the coupon below to:
Reader Service, FREEPOST, PO Box 236, Croydon, Surrey CR9 9EL.

Next month's Romances

Each month, you can chose from a world of variety in romance with Mills & Boon. These are the new titles to look out for next month.

ONCE BITTEN, TWICE SHY ROBYN DONALD

SAVING GRACE CAROLE MORTIMER

AN UNLIKELY ROMANCE BETTY NEELS

STORMY VOYAGE SALLY WENTWORTH

A TIME FOR LOVE AMANDA BROWNING

INTANGIBLE DREAM PATRICIA WILSON

IMAGES OF DESIRE ANNE BEAUMONT

OFFER ME A RAINBOW NATALIE FOX

TROUBLE SHOOTER DIANA HAMILTON

A ROMAN MARRIAGE STEPHANIE HOWARD

DANGEROUS COMPANY KAY GREGORY

DECEITFUL LOVER HELEN BROOKS

FOR LOVE OR POWER ROSALIE HENAGHAN

DISTANT SHADOWS ALISON YORK

FLORENTINE SPRING CHARLOTTE LAMB

STARSIGN

HUNTER'S HAREM ELEANOR REES